L(

~ West Series ~
Lauren & Chase
© 2013 Jill Sanders

Follow Jill online at:
Jill@JillSanders.com
http://JillSanders.com
Jill on Twitter
Jill on Facebook
Sign up for Jill's Newsletter

Dedication

To my cowboy

Many
Cowboy time
Jill Sanders

Summary

Lauren had been raised to not be afraid of anything, and she lived by that code, that is until her dad died and left everything in her hands. Now she's not only in charge of her two younger sisters, but she's running a full-blown Texas ranch. Caring for a thousand-acre ranch has its ups and downs, physically, mentally, and financially. All she is looking for is a little break. What she doesn't have time for is someone who will only complicate her life further.

Chase is back in his hometown. Helping his dad with his veterinary practice is high on his list. So is being with the lovely Lauren West. Years ago, he found a unique way to bind them together. Now all he has to do is prove to her that he's the right man to spend the rest of her life with.

Table of Contents

Dedication 1

Chapter One...12

Chapter Two..27

Chapter Three...45

Chapter Four...68

Chapter Five...81

Chapter Six...95

Chapter Seven...109

Chapter Eight...124

Chapter Nine..141

Chapter Ten..159

Chapter Eleven...172

Chapter Twelve...188

Chapter Thirteen...203

Chapter Fourteen..216

Chapter Fifteen...235

Chapter Sixteen..247

Epilogue 262

Taming Alex - Preview

....265

Chapter One...270

Other books by Jill Sanders.....................................285

About the Author..287

Jill Sanders

Loving Lauren

by
Jill Sanders

Jill Sanders

Prologue

Hot wind whirled around Lauren's skirt, causing it to fly up. She laughed as she twirled around. Stopping for a second to catch her breath, she looked over at her sisters, Alex and Haley. Alex's bright blonde head was pointed downward as she sat in the dirt, happily making a mud pile. Haley's dark curly hair lay in the grass as she watched the clouds rush by.

Lauren looked up at the sky and noticed that the clouds were going by very fast. Frowning a little, she decided that dancing some more while keeping her eyes glued to the sky might be fun. She twirled while watching everything rush by her, almost causing her to tumble over and fall.

Dancing in the fields was one of her greatest joys. Even though she had to babysit her younger sisters today, she didn't mind. For the most part, her sisters could entertain themselves. Lauren still had to carry Haley sometimes when her short legs got tired. She supposed that being four was tiring, though she couldn't remember ever being four. She thought she must have slept through her life until she turned five, when her first memories happened. Haley was always asleep, or lying down, like now. But Lauren was eight and she had enough energy to shake the roof off the barn, or so her Daddy always said.

The breeze moved the tall grass around them, making the field look as if it were dancing with her. She stopped to bow to her make-believe dance partner, a move she'd seen late one night when she had sneaked to the edge of the stairs. Her parents had been watching an old black-and-white movie and she could make out the screen if she tilted her head just right. The woman in the long white dress had bowed slowly while smiling at a tall gentlemen in a black suit and tie. They'd looked so wonderful. From that moment on, Lauren had wanted to dance. Every chance she had, she'd moved around like she'd watched the couple do, wishing her dress was longer so it would flow like the lady's had.

Taking a break, she looked off towards the house. The large three-story stone place sat like a beacon in the yellow fields. Its bright white pillars gleamed in the sunlight, at least when the clouds weren't shadowing the land. It was the only place she'd ever known as home. Her dad's dad had built the place a long, long time ago. Probably a zillion years ago. The outside looked new, and her dad did everything he could to keep the inside looking new, too. But Lauren knew some of the floorboards creaked when you walked on them. And the water only stayed hot long enough for her and her sisters to share a bath at night. But worst of all, she had blue carpet in her bedroom. Lauren hated blue. She'd begged her dad for new carpet, yellow preferably. Her dad told her it was blue because it used to be his room, and that it would have to stay blue until they could afford new carpet. Her room was perfect, except for the blue carpet. It was like a big wart on her room. Not that she'd ever gotten warts. Jenny Steven's had a wart once on her finger and she had to wear a My Little Pony Band-Aid over it. But during recess, Jenny had pulled the Band-Aid off and shown Lauren her wart. It was gross, all wet and puffy. So Lauren thought of her blue carpet as a wart on the face of her bedroom.

Looking at the house, she knew her mama was back in the kitchen making a feast for the church potluck tomorrow. Everyone was going to be there, even Dale Bennett. She didn't like Dale; he always pulled her hair and pushed her into the dirt, even when she was wearing her new church dress.

She knew that her mama was the best cook in the county. Or so her daddy always said.

Hearing a loud noise, she looked off towards the dark clouds that were forming over the hills. Her daddy was somewhere up in the hills, gathering the cows. She didn't know why they had to move the cows around all the time. It was still a mystery to her why they couldn't just stay here in the fields. There was plenty of tall grass to eat right here, close to the house. Another loud sound came from the hills. At first, Lauren thought it was a gunshot. She'd heard a lot of those growing up on the huge ranch, but then she turned her head a little and heard her mother screaming for them.

"Girls! Run, come quick!" Her mother stood in the front door, her apron flowing in the wind as her hands motioned for them to come to her.

"Come on. Mama wants us to run," Lauren told her sisters.

Alex stood and dusted off her hands and started skipping towards the house. Haley on the other hand didn't move.

"Come on, Haley, Mama wants us to run home." Another loud noise came from behind her and when she looked, the sky had turned black. Fear shot through her like a bolt of lightning. Without saying a word, Lauren grabbed up her baby sister and started running. Since her legs were longer than Alexis', she made it to her skipping sister and screamed for her to run faster. Halfway to the house, Lauren had to set Haley down. Her little sister had gained a few pounds and was too heavy for her to carry the entire way. Their mother wasn't in the doorway when they got there; instead, she was standing in the hallway.

"Quick, we have to get to the shelter." Her mother picked up Haley and started running towards the back door.

"Mama, Bear!" Haley screamed. "I want Bear!"

Their old deaf dog was lying by the fireplace, where he always stayed, taking a nap.

"Fine." Their mother set Haley down next to her and looked Lauren in the eyes. At this time,

Lauren could hear the wind rushing through the house. The sound was so loud that Haley covered her ears and started to cry. "Lauren, I want you to make sure you get your sisters into the shelter, like I taught you. Can you do that?"

Lauren remembered the drills Mama and Papa had put her through. Nodding her head, she grabbed her sisters' hands. "Yes, Mama."

"Good. Now run," her mother yelled over the noise, then she took off down the hallway to grab the dog as Lauren turned and started running, dragging her sisters behind her. When they got to the kitchen, Alex stopped. She pulled her hand out of Lauren's and started grabbing cookies that their mother had been baking.

"No, Alex, we have to go now." Lauren dropped Haley's hand and grabbed Alex by the shoulders, causing her to drop all the cookies.

"No, I'm gonna tell Mama." Alex started crying. Here in the back of the house the noise was even louder. She could see grass and leaves fly by the windows when she looked out.

"We have to get to the shelter, or Mama is going tell Daddy." That stopped her sister from picking up the dropped cookies. Lauren grabbed her hand and turned back to get Haley, but Haley was gone. Just then their mother came into the kitchen carrying the old dog.

"Where's Haley?" she screamed, as she held the

old dog in her arms.

"I don't know. She was just here. Then Alex—"

"Here, we don't have time for stories now. Take Bear and Alex and get to the shelter. Run girls, run!" Her mother pushed Bear into her arms. The dog looked small in her mother's arms, but in hers, he was heavy. She had to shift his fat body to make sure she didn't drop him. Alex ran to the back door and opened it. Hearing her mother's urgent tone, she must have understood that something bad was happening.

The girls rushed across the backyard through the high wind and the heavy rain that was falling. When they reached the storm shelter, Lauren had to set Bear down to open the big door. Alex grabbed Bear's collar, making sure he didn't run away as Lauren pushed the door open. Then Alex pulled Bear down the stairs as Lauren looked back towards the house. She could see a light go on in her sister's bedroom, then her mother's shadow crossed the window. Her mother bent down, and when she stood back up, Lauren could see that Haley was in her arms. She felt relieved until she looked up.

"Run, Mama!" Lauren screamed. The dark clouds circled above the house, and Lauren's little body froze to the spot outside the shelter. It seemed like hours later when her mother finally appeared at the back door holding Haley. Her sister's head was buried in her mother's apron.

"Get inside!" her mother screamed halfway across the backyard.

Lauren's feet became unglued and she rushed to the bottom of the stairs. Turning, she waited for her mother to reach the shelter door. She watched as her mother's dress flew sideways in the high winds. Haley was holding onto her apron tightly.

Then everything slowed down in Lauren's mind. Her mother, a few steps from the doorway, looked up quickly, then turned her head and looked right at her. Lifting Haley high, she threw her into the open doorway. Haley fell down the stairs, and her little body hit Lauren's with enough force that it knocked them down. Haley's body shook as she cried, still clutching a piece of their mother's apron, which had been ripped from her shoulders. Lauren quickly got up and stood on the floor of the shelter, looking up into the doorway. She watched in terror as the ferocious winds ripped her mother from the doorway and swept her into the darkness.

Jill Sanders

Chapter One

Ten years later...

*L*auren looked down at the grave as a tear slipped down her nose. It was a week before her nineteenth birthday, and she watched as her father's closest friends lowered his casket into the ground. She heard her sisters crying beside her and blindly reached over and took both of their hands. It had been two days since she'd found her father lying on his bedroom floor. She'd done everything she'd known to try and save him, but she'd been too late. She'd do anything to go back and somehow get to the house earlier that sunny day.

Closing her eyes, she could remember her father's face, his kindness, the way he moved and smelled, and the way he talked. Everything about the man had told his daughter's that he loved them, that he'd do anything for them. They'd lost their mother ten years ago; their father had picked up the pieces and raised three girls on his own. They had all missed their mother, but thanks to their father, they had grown up knowing that they were loved. They had never gone to bed hungry, dirty, or without a bedtime story.

If the food had been a little burnt or a little odd tasting, the girls never complained. Even when Alex's costume for the school play had turned out looking more like a green leaf than a tree, she hadn't complained. When Lauren had finally hit the age to legally drive, she'd taken it upon herself to drive her sisters to and from school and any other after school functions they'd been involved in, even if it meant forgoing her own social life.

The guilt had always played in the back of her mind. *If I had just watched Haley better. If I had just kept holding her hand, Mama would be here today.*

The school had offered the girls counseling, but Lauren had just sat through it and had told the older woman who had been assigned to counsel her what she'd wanted to hear. Not once did she hint that it was her fault that their mother was gone. Not once did she confide in anyone that she was to blame.

When her father was in the ground, she closed her eyes and lifted her face to the sky. The spring

Texas air felt wonderful. She knew that in a little over a month, the breeze would be hot enough to steam the tears that were falling down her face. The cool wind would stop and be replaced by stillness and heat. But for now, she enjoyed the smell of the grass growing, the flowers blooming, and the sight of the cherry trees that were planted around the small cemetery. Her father had always loved the spring. He'd been looking forward to helping her plant a new flower garden near the back of the house.

Now who was she going to plant flowers with? She opened her eyes and looked at Alexis. Her blonde hair was tied up in a simple bun at the base of her neck. Her black skirt and gray shirt were in complete contrast to her sister's normal attire. Even though Alex had just turned sixteen, her wild side had been on the loose for the last two years. So much so that it had started eating up a lot of Lauren's and their father's time.

"Your sister is going to be the death of me. Mark my words, Lauren. Someday you're going to walk in and she'll be standing over my cold body, complaining about the fact that she can't have a pair of hundred-dollar jeans."

In fact, Alex hadn't been home that day. She'd stayed the night at a friend's house that entire weekend.

Lauren looked over at Haley. She was too young to remember their mother. And even though they'd never talked about it, she knew her sister was a little jealous of the fact that Lauren and Alex could both remembered her.

As the minister, a longtime family friend, was saying his closing, Lauren looked down at her father's final resting place. What was she going to do now? How were they going to live without him?

Her shoulders sank a little as she walked forward and tossed a white rose into the hole, onto her father's casket. When she turned and stepped away, she looked off to the distance. West of here was Saddleback Ranch, their home for as long as she could remember. It had been handed down for three generations now.

Straightening her shoulders and looking off to the distance, she knew in her heart that she'd do anything—anything—to keep it. To keep her and her sisters together. On their land. Like her father and mother would have wanted her to do.

After shaking the hands of and hugging almost everyone in the small three-thousand-person strong community, she stood outside her truck talking briefly with Grant Holton Sr., her father's lawyer and one of his best friends. Mr. Holton was tall and very broad chested. She'd heard once that he and her father had played football together.

She looked over as Dr. Graham and his son, Chase, walked up to them. Dr. Graham had been the ranch's veterinarian. Every animal on her land was healthy thanks to the older man who walked forward and shook her hand with a firm grip. Chase had been a year ahead of her in school. They'd grown up together and had even gone to a couple dances together in high school and had shared a few stolen kisses behind the bleachers. But then he'd graduated and she'd seen less and less of him.

Chase was tall like his father. It looked like he'd tried to grease back his bushy mass of black hair for the ceremony. She'd always loved pushing her hands into his thick hair. His dark brown eyes stared at her with sincere concern and grief, much like his father's did now.

"Lauren." Dr. Graham shook her hand, then Mr. Holton's.

Mr. Holton nodded, then turned towards her. "I know this isn't the time to think about your future or the ranch's future, but maybe we can meet tomorrow. Just the three of us. There are a few details I need to go over with you."

At that moment, realization hit her—she was the head of the house. She was now in charge of a thousand-acre ranch. In charge of her sisters. In charge of the cattle, the horses, everything. She must have paled a little, because Chase stepped forward and took her elbow. "Are you okay?" he whispered.

She wanted to shove his arm away and scream. "No! I'm not okay, you idiot. Everything is ruined!

I have no family left." But instead, she nodded and swayed a little, causing him to move his other arm around her waist. "Dad," Chase said, looking towards his father.

"Quite right, we apologize." The older man cleared his throat, looking towards his friend.

"No," Lauren blinked. If she wanted to keep the three of them on her family's land, she would just have to step up a little more. Remember, she told herself, keep your sisters together and do whatever it takes to stay on your family's land. "If you want, I'm heading back to the house now. We can meet in say"—she looked at her watch as Chase dropped his arm—"an hour?"

Dr. Graham and Mr. Holton nodded their heads in unison. She could see the questions in their eyes. Lauren turned when she spotted her sisters walking towards her. She walked stiffly around to the driver's side of her truck, her shoulders square. As they drove away in silence, she looked back and saw the three men standing there. A shiver rolled down her back and she knew at that moment that everything was going to change.

The drive to the ranch wasn't a long one. It sat almost ten miles outside of town, but the roads were always empty and the highway stretched in a straight line. When they passed the old iron gate with Saddleback Ranch overhead, she felt a little peace settle in her bones. There, in the distance, stood the three-story house she'd always known and loved. It had taken some bangs in its time. The tornado that had claimed their mother had torn the roof right off the massive place. The old red barn had been flattened back then as well. They'd lost a dozen horses and two of the farmhand houses. Thank goodness her father and the men had been in the hills that day, or they might have been caught up in the storm as well. But the barn and farmhands' houses had been rebuilt. The house had gotten a shiny new roof, along with a new paint job and some new windows panes to replace the ones that had blown out. After her father replaced the storm cellar's door, no one talked about that day anymore.

Lauren stopped the truck in front of the barn, and Haley jumped out and ran through the massive doors. Alex turned and looked at Lauren.

"Don't worry. I'll go talk to her." Lauren patted her sister's thigh and got out of the truck. Dingo, the family dog, an Australian shepherd mix, rushed up to Lauren and jumped on her dress. "No, down." She pushed the dog off, but she followed her into the dark barn.

Outside, the sun had warmed her, but here in the darkness of the barn, the coolness seeped into her bones. She rubbed her arms with her hands as she walked forward to climb the old stairs that led to the second floor, where she knew her sister would be.

The loft was huge, taking up three quarters of

the barn, but Lauren knew Haley's hiding places and walked right to her sister. Haley was stretched out on the soft hay, her best Sunday dress fanned out around her. She was face down and crying like there was no tomorrow. Lauren walked over and sat next to her. She pulled her into her arms and cried with her.

Less than an hour later, Lauren had changed into her work clothes and stood at the door to greet Mr. Holton, Dr. Graham, and, to her surprise, Chase. The four of them walked into her father's large office and she shut the glass doors behind her. Taking a large breath, she turned to face the room.

"Please, have a seat." She motioned for the three men to sit as she walked around her father's massive desk and sat in his soft leather chair. She'd done it a hundred times, but this time it felt different.

"Your father was a great man," Mr. Holton started. "He was our best friend." He looked at Dr. Graham, and the other man nodded his head in agreement. "We could postpone this meeting for —"

"No, please." Lauren straightened her shoulders.

"Very well." Mr. Holton pulled out a file from his briefcase. "As you know, I am your father's lawyer. John, here"—he nodded to Dr. Graham —"well, he has a stake in what we need to discuss.

That's why I invited him along."

"Continue," Lauren said when she thought Mr. Holton had lost his nerve. She knew it was bad news; she could see it clearly on both man's faces.

"Well, after that day"—Mr. Holton cleared his throat and shifted in his seat—"after we lost your mother, Richard took out some loans."

"Mr. Holton, how much did my father owe the bank?" She wanted the bottom line. Holding her breath, she waited.

"Well, that's the tricky part. You see, Richard didn't trust in banks all that much." The two older men looked between themselves. "Maybe this will explain it better." He set the file on the desk in front of her.

She opened the file with shaky fingers. There, in her father's handwriting, was her future.

I, Richard West, being of sound body and mind, do solemnly promise to pay back the total sum of $100,000.00 to Johnathan Graham Sr. and Grant Holton II. If anything should happen to me, the proceeds of my ranch, Saddleback Ranch, would go to both men in equal amounts until paid back in full. They would have a say in the running of the ranch until said amount was paid in full.

It had been dated and signed by her father, John Graham, and Grant Holton Sr. over ten years ago.

"I understand your concerns." She looked up from the paper. "As head of the house now, I will fulfill my father's obligations."

"Well, that's all well and good." Dr. Graham smiled. "But, well, we had an understanding between the three of us. If anything happened to him and we saw that you three or the ranch was in any jeopardy, we'd step in and run this place until we saw fit."

Lauren listened as the men told her the scheme the three of them—her father, Mr. Holton and Dr. Graham—had come up with ten years ago in case anything like this should happen. How they'd take over the running of the land, the handling of the finances, even deciding how to deal with her and her sisters. She was being pushed out before she'd even had the chance to try and run things her way. She'd practically raised her sisters, and now these two men wanted to take control of everything, even her. Her heart sank upon hearing this news. She asked for some time to think about it and the men apologized and quickly excused themselves.

After the older men had driven away, Chase stayed behind and offered her another option. The next day Lauren stood in front of the courthouse in Tyler, wearing her Sunday best. She knew her life would never be the same again after that day.

Seven years later...

Chase stood in the middle of the street and took a deep breath. He was finally home. It wasn't that he'd been avoiding the place, or that he hadn't had the will to return, but life had led him down a twisted path. He was happy that he'd finally ended up back here, at least for now. A car horn honked at him, and he waved and moved from the center of the road. Walking up the stone steps to his father's building, he realized that the old green place had never looked better. He knew the money he'd been sending home over the last nine years had helped with fixing up the clinic.

When he opened the front door, the bell above the door chimed and he smiled.

"Morning, how can I—" Cheryl, his father's receptionist, stood slowly. "Son of a..."

"Now, Cheryl, you know you're not supposed to say that around here." He walked forward and received her welcome hug. The woman almost engulfed him, but he smiled and took the beating as she patted his back hard. Her arms were like vices, but her front was soft and she smelled just like he remembered, like chocolate and wet puppies. The odd mix of aromas had always warmed his spirits.

"What are you doing back in town?" she asked. She gasped. "Does your father know?" She looked toward the back room.

He shook his head. "I wanted to surprise him." He smiled.

Her smile slipped a little. "Well, you sure will." Then she bit her bottom lip and he knew something was up.

"Spill." He took her shoulders before she could turn away.

"What?" She tried to look innocent.

"Cheryl, how long have I known you?"

She smiled. "Going on twenty-eight years next June." He smiled. Cheryl always did remembered his birthday.

"And in all that time, I've come to know that when you bite your bottom lip, you have something you're trying to hide. So..."—he motioned with his hand—"spill."

She crossed her arms over her chest. "Fine. It's just your father's health. I know he hasn't mentioned it over the phone to you."

"What about it?" Chase began to get worried and felt like rushing to the back room to check up on his dad. Cheryl had never mentioned anything personal about his father's health in their conversations. Neither had his father.

"Well, he injured his leg a while back." She twisted her shirtfront.

"And?" He waited.

"And, well, he's walking with a cane now," she blurted out, just as his father walked through the back door.

"Thank you, Cheryl. That will be enough out of you." His father smiled. Sure enough, his father was leaning on a black cane. "Well, boy?" He held out his arm. "Don't make me hobble over to you for that hug."

Chase rushed across the room and gave his old man a bear hug like he always had, noticing that his father was not only skinnier, but felt frailer. He had a million questions he wanted to ask, but knew his father wouldn't answer until he was good and ready.

"Come on back here, boy. Tell me what you've been up to." His father started walking towards the back and Chase watched him hobble. Then his father turned. "Are you back to stay?"

"Yes," Chase said absentmindedly. He hadn't meant to stay, had he?

"Good." His father turned into his office and took a seat, setting the cane down beside him. Chase sat in the chair across from him, waiting.

"Well, I suppose I should tell you, you couldn't have come home at a better time. I'm retiring."

"What?" Chase sat up. His father raised his hands, holding off the million questions he had.

"Yes, at the end of the year. I've been kicked one too many times." His father smiled. "This old body doesn't want to work like it used to. I was going to give you a call later this month."

"Dad?" He looked at him.

"I know, I know. I told you I'd never retire, but..." he looked down at his leg. "The doctors are telling me I have to be off this damned leg for six hours a day. Six! You and I both know that in this line of work you'd be lucky to sit for five minutes a day."

Chase smiled. "I guess it's a good thing I'm home, then."

His father smiled and nodded his head. "What do you say we go grab some lunch? I'm buying."

Fairplay, Texas, had one place to sit and eat. Mama's Diner, a huge brown barn that had been turned into a restaurant, had been the best place to eat in two counties since as far back as Chase could remember. Even now the place looked new and smelled like greasy burgers.

His father took his usual booth. It almost made Chase laugh, knowing the man never sat in a different spot. Even if someone was in it, he'd stand and wait until the table was cleared. There were new menus and he took his time looking over the list of new items.

"How are you today, beautiful?" his father asked the waitress when she stopped by.

Chase looked up and stared into the most beautiful green eyes he'd ever seen. Her hair was longer than before, and her dark curls hung just below the most perfect breasts he'd ever had the pleasure of being up against. She was tall and limber and he could remember the softness of every curve he'd been allowed to feel. She looked down at him like he was in her way and he started coughing. He couldn't explain how it happened, but he was choking on air. Nothing was getting through to his lungs or to his brain. Finally, she smacked his back hard, and he took a deep breath. He stood and grabbed Lauren's arm and demanded in a low voice, "What the hell are you doing working here?"

Jill Sanders

Chapter Two

$\mathcal{L}$auren jerked her arm away and stared back at Chase. Two minutes earlier she'd gotten the shock of her life as she'd watched him and his father walk across the street from the clinic. She'd almost dropped the tray carrying Mrs. Jenkins's spaghetti. Luckily, she'd learned to handle unexpected circumstances and recovered quite quickly.

Maybe he's just visiting, she kept saying over and over in her head. He was a lot taller than she remembered, and she had to crane her neck to glare into his chocolate eyes. She slowly crossed her arms over her chest and said, "I don't see how it's any of your business where I work." She dismissed him and turned to his father and gave him a huge smile. "How are you doing today, Doc?"

"Oh, just fine, just fine. My boy's back in town to stay, and I have a hankering for one of your sloppy joe's and some sweet tea, please." The older man smiled up at her, then turned to frown at his son, who was still standing beside her and glaring at her. "Sit down, boy. You're making a spectacle of yourself."

Chase sat without taking his eyes off her. She wrote down the doc's order, then turned and gave Chase a big smile. "What'll you have?"

"An answer to my question." He crossed his arms and smiled a little. The dimple at the side of his mouth winked and for a split second, she forgot to breath. How had he grown so handsome? Sure, he'd been good looking in school, but nothing like he was now. His hair was a lot shorter, and it looked like he'd dropped ten pounds. He was very lean and had a bunch of new muscles. She was impressed with the ones she could see on his arms as he crossed them over his chest, which led her to look at his chest. It was wider than before. She could see the tension in his shoulder muscles and wondered what they'd look like, what they'd feel like. Shaking her head, she walked away without saying another word.

When she made it to the back, she leaned against the wall and took several deep breaths. What was Chase doing back in town? Why couldn't he just leave her alone? She felt herself hyperventilating. Then the words, "My boy's back in town to stay," hit her and her hands began shaking. What did his return mean for her and the ranch?

"You okay, honey?" Jamella asked. Her boss was fifty years older and about a hundred pounds heavier than she was. She was Mama in every sense. Her family had owned Mama's Diner since coming to Fairplay from Louisiana when Jamella was ten. Now, after raising her own children, who had all quickly vacated the small town, she was Mama to everyone under the age of thirty. She knew everyone's business, and most important, knew how to keep a secret.

"Chase is back." It came out as a whisper.

"What? Why is dat boy back?" She poked her head through the window. "Hmm hmph." Jamella crossed her arms over her chest and nodded her head once. "It's 'bout time he came back."

"Jamella! He's baaack!" Lauren drug out the last word as if to make her point.

"Well, you knew this day was coming, child. I guess it's time to put on your big girl panties and go out there and see what he want." She shook her head and pushed Lauren towards the door.

"Thanks," she mumbled as she half-fell, half-walked out the swinging doors. Lauren turned to the window to see Jamella and Willard, the cook, looking out the order window. Jamella waved her hand towards Chase and mouthed, "Go on, child."

Lauren straightened her shoulders and turned. Walking up to their table, she looked down her nose at Chase and asked in a clear voice, "What is it you want?"

He looked up at her and a smile slowly formed on his lips. She felt heat rushing to her face. He leaned back and crossed his arms. "Dad tells me you fill in for your sister here every now and then."

She moved her chin up a fraction. It really wasn't any of his business what she did with her time or money. She looked down at him, waiting.

"He also tells me things are running smoothly at the ranch." Her eyes narrowed and she could feel her blood beginning to boil. "I suppose I'll head out there later this week, just to check up...on the livestock." She slowly crossed her arms and felt her face turn red with anger. "You know, since I'll be taking over dad's practice at the end of the year." His smile got bigger.

She looked over to his dad and frowned. "You're retiring?" He nodded and she felt her heart sink. That meant that...she looked over at Chase quickly and his smile dropped a little. That meant that Chase *was* here to stay. Her shoulders slumped a little. Feeling defeated, she said. "Yes, I suppose you'll want to stop by the ranch. I'll be there all week." She knew she sounded a little deflated, but she couldn't help it. She felt that way.

After her shift was over, she drove home and tried her best to hide the fear she felt inside so that her sisters wouldn't see. Before going inside, she walked into the barn and stayed there until she felt like she could control her fear. She walked over to Tanner's stall and leaned her head against his tan one while stroking his blond mane.

"Why does everything have to be so complicated?" she asked the horse.

She heard a noise behind her and when she jolted and turned, she saw Hewitt, her foreman's nephew, whom she'd hired on a few weeks back.

"Pardon, miss. I didn't know you was in here." He shuffled his boots and nodded his head. Still, his eyes bore into her, making her feel a little uncomfortable.

Hewitt was a good fifteen years younger and two times larger than Jimmy, the man that had been her foreman since her father had run the ranch. She'd only seen Hewitt a few times and each time his shirt was dirty and untucked, and his jeans had holes in them and looked like they could use a good washing. His hair looked like he'd greased it back with something dark, causing it to look constantly wet. She knew that he and a few other hands smoked, and she didn't mind as long as they didn't do it anywhere near the barn or house, but he stank of cigarettes. But Jimmy had vouched for him so she'd hired him and eleven other men this year to help around the ranch. She only employed six men year-round. The others came and went depending on the ranch needs.

"I was just checking on the horses. Good night." She nodded as she walked by him. When she reached the barn door, she took in a deep breath of fresh air and headed towards the back door of the house. Haley was sitting at the kitchen table watching the news on the old TV set when she walked in.

"Where's Alex?" Lauren dropped her bag on the counter and leaned against it, then watched Haley lift her shoulders and drop them again, not removing her eyes from the set. Lauren took just a second to watch the news, then turned and started pulling out items to make for dinner. She knew that if she didn't cook, her sisters would grab just about anything, usually cold cereal or leftover pizza someone had ordered for lunch. Haley occasionally got the idea to cook, but Alex steered clear of the kitchen altogether.

Family dinners were a ritual she tried to keep for her sisters. Even if she couldn't cook every night, she at least tried for a few nights a week. Plus, cooking always gave her time to think. On more than one occasion tonight, Chase Graham's image popped into her mind. She was worried what his moving back into town meant, and knowing he was planning on stopping by the ranch later this week set her nerves on high alert.

"Hey." Alex came in the back door a few minutes later. Her shirt was untucked and she had hay in her hair. Her sister leaned against the counter top, picked up an apple, and bit into it.

Lauren looked out the window and saw a truck spitting up dust as it flew down their drive, heading back towards town. "Is that Travis Nolan's truck I see driving away?" She turned and glared at her sister. She didn't like him coming onto her land anymore, and she was sure he was speeding away since he'd seen her truck parked out front.

Alex just shrugged her shoulders. "He was just returning my stuff and he wanted to talk to me. You know we broke it off weeks ago."

Lauren walked over and plucked a piece of hay from her sister's blonde hair, then held it up for her to see. "Did you two do a lot of 'talking' in the hayloft?"

Haley snickered behind them, causing both her sisters to glare at her. "Sorry." Haley quickly looked away.

Lauren walked over and picked up the knife and started chopping items to go into their salad. Alex crossed her arms over her chest and glared. "Wasn't that Chase Graham I saw in town earlier today?" Lauren stopped chopping the vegetables and looked over at her sister.

"Doc's retiring."

"What?" Haley jumped out of her seat. "Doc

can't retire!" She walked over and took a carrot from the chopping block and bit into it.

"He is, and Chase is taking over." Lauren went back to making the salad as Haley pulled the dishes out of the cupboard and set them on the table. Alex stood there and watched her sisters. "Chase is going to be stopping by later this week."

"I don't like anyone looking at the herd except Doc." Haley dumped the silverware on the table and sat back down. As far as setting the table, Lauren knew that was as nice as it was going to get around here, at least with her sisters helping.

"I think we should give Chase a chance," Alex put in. She had a wicked smile on her face and Lauren immediately knew what was coming next. "After all, he is still single. According to Mary Beth, he's been living in upstate New York for the last four years. Before that he was in Dallas. And according to Mary Beth, who heard it from Cheryl Lynn, who got it straight from Chase's daddy, he hasn't been seeing anyone serious. So..." Lauren rolled her eyes, wishing her sister's speech was over already. "Now that Travis and I have called things off, maybe I'll put on my Sunday best and give Chase a visit." Alex pulled her shorter hair back into a band and walked over to sit at the table.

Alex sure knew how to push Lauren's buttons, but she wasn't going to let it get to her this time. Lauren had been sideswiped already once today; there was no way she was letting her sister get under her skin. With her back turned towards her sisters, she smiled. "Go right ahead. I think you two would make a very handsome couple. At least we wouldn't be seeing so much of Travis anymore."

She heard Haley chuckle and try to cover it up with a cough.

The next morning, Lauren rode Tanner, her three-year-old gelding, out of the barn, her tools for the day packed up in her saddlebag. She knew it was going to be a long day when she started riding the fence and saw that a large branch from an oak had taken out a chunk of the front fence. Pulling Tanner to a stop and tying him to another branch under the oak, she walked the fence and assessed the damage. Luckily, it wasn't all that bad. She decided she could do most of the repairs without heading back to the house to get the chainsaw or needing any of the men to help her.

She put on leather gloves from her bag, grabbed the wire cutters, and got to work. Dingo ran up to her and lay at her feet and Lauren started talking to her. She was enjoying the fact that it wasn't quite summer yet. The cool breeze helped a little as she worked under the hot sun. She'd just finished repairing the largest section when a shadow fell over her. Spinning around, she almost screamed as she took a step back and fell right into the barbed wire, backside down.

Chase pulled the old mare's mouth open and looked at her teeth. He shook his head and then scratched between the horse's ears, causing her to push her head farther into his hands. He laughed and continued rubbing the mare's coarse hair. When he walked out of the barn, he strolled across the yard towards Edward.

"Well?"

"I don't like the look of Betty's teeth. She's got an abnormal wear pattern. I'd like to come back and bring my dentistry kit."

"Is that why she's bleeding from the mouth?" Edward asked, eager for the answer.

"Looks like. One of her teeth is scraping the side of her cheek every time she bites down. I can fix it tomorrow around eight, if that's alright with you?"

"Yeah, sure. She's been a good old girl. I sure hate to see her in pain." Edward looked off towards the barn. "I know I've only got about another year with her, but she deserves to grow old without the hassle of losing all her teeth, unlike me." The old man smiled, showing a huge gap. Chase laughed.

As he drove away from Edward's ranch, he

figured he was so close to Saddleback Ranch that he'd stop by. He hadn't expected to see Lauren out in the field, putting up a barbed wire fence. He parked his truck at the edge of the drive and started walking up the grassy hill toward her. Her horse, a beautiful sand-colored gelding, stood in the shade of an old oak a few yards away. Lauren's hat shielded her from the sun, but he could see that her shirt had soaked through with sweat, letting him know she'd been out there working for a while.

He saw a black and brown dog lying by her feet and when he approached, the dog looked up at him, then laid her head back down, closing her eyes. Lauren was talking to the dog, like it was a human.

"Can you believe she said that? Like I'd care if she had anything to do with the man. For all I care, Alex can take Chase Graham and..." His shadow fell over her and she spun around quickly. The wire stretcher in her hands swung out towards him, and then she fell backwards into the fence, screaming. He grabbed for her, but was still too far away to save her from falling right into the fence.

"Don't move!" he demanded as he rushed over and tried to hold the wire so it wouldn't wrap around her legs. She was already trying to stand, pushing at the wire with her gloved hands. "I said stop it. You're only going to get yourself caught up in it more." Her hat had fallen off and now the dog was barking and chasing it like it was all a big game.

"Leave me alone. I can pull myself out of here all by myself," she hissed as he put his boot on one of the wires and held it away from her. He could see a large rip in the back of her jeans. He stopped for just a flash to admire the soft skin before stepping on the other wire, putting his hands under her arms, and pulling her up with one quick motion. She let out a gasp as her feet flew off the ground, then he set her down and pulled them a few steps away from the fence.

She stood there, leaning into him, her breathing ragged as she looked up into his eyes. For a second her green eyes dropped and focused on his lips, then they moved up to his eyes again. He could see the moment she regained her wits, after blinking a few times.

"What are you doing walking up and scaring me like that?" She pushed away from him and tried to look at her backside, almost walking in circles to see the tear in her jeans.

He almost laughed at the image she made, but then he saw the gash on the back of her thigh. He dropped down on his knees in front of her and took her hips in his hands to stop her movement. Then he turned her around. "Here, let me look at that." He pulled her back a step so she was closer and then opened the rip in her jeans a little more with his fingertips. There was a nasty cut that crossed the back of her left thigh, causing her pale skin to pucker and turn a nasty color of red.

"What do you..." She started to pull away, but he held her hips in place and moved her back another step, towards him and the light.

"Shhh." He leaned closer and opened the rip in her jeans even a little farther, trying to get a better look at the gash. He let out a breath of air when he realized she wouldn't need stitches. Looking over, he made sure that her right leg had gone unscathed. Her jeans were uncut and as far as he could tell, the damage had been limited to just the one leg. "If you think you can walk to my truck, I'll take care of this. Clean it up." He stood and looked at her as she glanced over her shoulder at him. He nodded to where he'd parked his truck along the driveway.

She pulled out of his grip and walked a few steps. He could see that it pained her to do so, but she held her head up high and looked down at him. "I certainly don't need your help. I can take care of myself."

He slowly crossed his arms over his chest. She was being ridiculous. "Really? I suppose you're going to ride back to the house like that, and tend to that cut all by yourself." He smiled and waited as she looked off towards her horse, then off to the house in the distance.

"I'll walk." Her chin came up and she crossed her arms over her chest, mimicking his stance.

"So it's come to this? You won't even take help from me? Even when I'm partially at fault?"

"Partially?" She uncrossed her arms and took a step towards him and her eyes narrowed.

"Well, if you'd been listening, instead of talking to the dog about my love life, you would have heard my truck and known that I was coming up behind you. It took me at least a full minute to climb the hill there." He pointed behind him.

Her chin dropped. "I wasn't...I didn't..." She stood there and glared at him. "I wasn't talking about your love life."

His eyebrows shot up. "Really? I seem to remember you saying, and I quote, "For all I care, Alex can take Chase Graham." I'd like to know exactly what you intend for me to do with your little sister?" He smiled at her, knowing he'd hit a sore spot. Her chin came up and she glared back at him.

"For all I care, you can go to hell and back with her." She started marching towards her horse, and the flap in her jeans showed her exposed skin and the nasty cut.

Guilt hit him. "Lauren!" he called out, chasing after her. "Wait. I'm sorry. Really, let me fix you up. It's the least I can do." He pulled her to a stop under the shade of the oak.

"Because you're partially to blame?" She crossed her arms again and tried to pull out of his light grip.

"Yes." His smile was quick. He wanted to tell

her that he just wanted another look at the milky white skin on the back of her thigh, but knew better than to push his luck.

She chewed her bottom lip and he watched the motion as if hypnotized.

"Fine," she finally said and started walking more slowly towards his truck. He could see that the adrenalin had finally worn off and she was fully experiencing the pain.

He helped her walk to his truck, took out his medical bag, and then pulled down the tailgate. "You'd be better just leaning over." He motioned for her. She looked at him, then looked up and down the dirt road, making sure the coast was clear.

"Fine, but make it quick." She chewed her lip as she leaned over a little.

"You're going to have to bend over a lot more. Come on, Lauren, stick that beautiful bottom in the air." He chuckled when she glared over her shoulder at him. "I'll behave." He held back a laugh.

She closed her eyes, turned her head, then ducked down. He pulled out a cotton swab from his bag and started cleaning the cut.

"You're lucky. It doesn't look like you'll need stitches." She hissed when the antiseptic touched the open skin. He quickly bent closer and blew on the cut, trying to ease the pain. She froze. He froze.

Then he said, "Sorry," under his breath. It was like someone had kicked him in the chest, being this close to her, seeing the perfect skin that he'd exposed through the hole in her jeans.

Just then, a car horn honked, causing them both to jump. He'd been so busy, he hadn't heard someone drive up behind them. Lauren quickly straightened and turned around, putting her hands behind her back. Her face was bright red. Her hair was in a tangled mess, and wisps of dark curls were pulled out of her long braid, falling around her face. She looked as if she'd just been caught with her pants down. He chuckled. In a way, he supposed, she had.

He turned and watched Alexis step out of a small red sedan. "Well, well." She closed her door with a flurry and started slowly walking towards them. "Look what the cat dragged in."

Lauren's younger sister was nothing like her; in fact, they were complete opposites. Alex's bright blonde hair twinkled in the daylight, but he preferred seeing the darker highlights in Lauren's hair as the sun hit it. Alex was also the only sister with dark brown eyes and a much smaller stature. Not that Lauren and Haley were big, just better built in his opinion. Lauren had more of the curves that he admired most.

Alex was wearing her uniform from the diner. The blouse was opened dangerously low, and the skirt was a few inches higher than the one Lauren had worn the other day. Alex also wore heeled boots instead of black tennis shoes.

"Afternoon." He nodded, then looked back at Lauren. He watched as her eyes darted around, avoiding his.

"Chase was just fixing me up. I fell into the fence." She turned and showed her sister the rip in her jeans.

"Oh!" Alex rushed forward, showing true sisterly concern. "Are you hurt bad?"

"No, she'll live," he jumped in, thankful that Lauren hadn't mentioned that he'd been to blame.

"That's good." Alex relaxed a little.

Just then the dog came running up to Lauren, her hat in its mouth, and its tail wagging a million miles an hour.

"Thank you, Dingo. That was very kind of you." He found it funny that she talked to the dog like a human. He watched her wince with pain as she bent over and took her hat from the dog's mouth. Then the dog walked over and sat at Chase's feet. He bent down and pet her. "Well, hello, Dingo. It's very nice to meet such a wonderful helper." The dog rolled over and he started rubbing her belly.

"She's not that big of a helper since she didn't bark when you were sneaking up on me," Lauren said.

"I didn't sneak." He stood back up and crossed his arms over his chest, smiling at her.

"You most certainly did." Lauren put her hands on her hips.

"Well." Alex backed up a little. "I can see you two have everything under control here. I'll see you back at the house." Alex walked back to her car quickly and drove away.

Chase didn't spare her another glance, but walked right up to Lauren. "Do you know that you are absolutely beautiful when you're mad?" He brushed a strand of her hair away from her face. He'd meant to throw her off balance, but hadn't counted on the desire that had bubbled up inside him.

Chapter Three

$\mathcal{L}$auren couldn't seem to breathe. She couldn't move either. She heard her sister's car drive away and her heart refused to slow down. How had she let it get this far? Finally, she blinked a few times then turned and started marching up the hill towards Tanner without glancing behind her. She heard him right behind her, but didn't stop to turn around since she didn't feel like arguing. All she wanted was to be left alone.

When she reached the shade of the tree, she turned on him and pointed at his chest. "Why are you here?"

"I told you that I would stop by and check up on the stock. Since I'm taking over for my—"

"No, why are you here?" She took a step closer to him and looked up into his eyes. "I've been paying you—"

"This has nothing to do with that." He took her shoulders in his hands, gripping her tightly. She saw a flash of anger cross his face for a second, then it was gone. "I don't want your money."

"Then what? Why? Are you planning on moving in?"

"Moving in?" He looked at her like she was crazy. "Why would I move in?"

"Because we're..." She just couldn't bring herself to say it. Closing her eyes, she held her breath.

"Married?" he suggested, and her eyes flew open.

"Technically, yes." She tried to pull away.

He smiled. "I suppose I could call in the loan, so to speak. Move into the house and have you in my bed at night, but that would be going against my word."

She let out a sigh of relief.

"But it has been a little cramped at my dad's place. Since you mention it, I suppose I could move into one of the hand's houses."

She felt all the blood leave her head. She actually reached out to steady herself by holding onto Tanner's mane. The horse nuzzled his face into her chest, almost knocking her over. Chase reached over and took her shoulders to steady her.

"Is the possibility of me living on your land that scary?" He looked down into her eyes, waiting for an answer.

At least he'd said *her* land. She shook her head. How could she tell him that she didn't want anyone, mainly her sisters, to find out what she'd done seven years ago? What she'd had to do in order to save her land, her sisters, everything. It wasn't as if her decision had been a huge burden on her. At least it hadn't been up until now.

Seven years ago, it had been a different story. Chase had just received a scholarship to college in Dallas and was leaving Fairplay. There was a huge possibility that he wouldn't return for years, and at that point, she'd actually believed she could handle him when he did come home. Beside, she'd spent the last six years doing everything she could to pay him back, including working part time at the diner when she could pick up a shift. Now she only had a few more payments before she would have paid him off. Then she could have discreetly asked for a divorce, settling the matter once and for all. She hadn't planned on him coming home and moving into her ranch hand's house. On her land. Well, she thought, biting her lip, it is technically one-third his, still. It had been so since he'd used the inheritance he'd gotten from his grandmother to save her from her father's debt.

She had only agreed because he'd cornered her after the older men had left. His deal had sounded too good to pass up. He'd promised no interference with her methods of running the ranch, a promise she hadn't gotten from his father and Mr. Holton. He'd also promised no interference with her personal life. Chase had made it all sound so easy. He'd said there was no need to pay him back, and she'd jumped at the chance to be free to run the ranch herself. But a year later, she'd had a change of heart and had started sending him checks to pay him back. He hadn't cashed them, so she'd started sending him money orders, which he had quickly returned. So she'd marched down to the local bank and had opened a joint checking and savings account. She only ever dealt with the bank manager, Mr. Billings, who promised to never mention a word to anyone about the account that was under the names Lauren A. and Johnathan Chase Graham II. She had started making monthly deposits and sent Chase receipts every month. She's been satisfied that she'd won the small battle as she marked off in her bank book how much she had left to pay back.

But now, she looked up into Chase's chocolate eyes and wondered if he too had had a change of heart. Maybe he wanted to come back and take over running the ranch? She blinked a few times and decided that would happen over her cold body. Straightening herself to her full height, she tried to brush off his arms, but he kept hold of her and actually started to pull her closer.

"I'm not afraid of you," she said to reiterate her point. It didn't help that it came out as a whisper.

He smiled slightly, showing her the dimple at the side of his mouth, then his hand came up and pushed away a strand of hair that had blown in her face. She felt herself start to shake and took a step back. She hadn't been touched like this since...well, since he'd kissed her on the day they'd signed the wedding license at the courthouse over seven years ago.

"Don't," she said.

"Why? Do I make you nervous?" He was so close, she could see every long eyelash.

She shook her head. She was too out of breath to say anything else. Feeling her heart beating fast, she thought for just a moment that it would jump right out of her chest.

"Good." He leaned down, slowly. If she had wanted to, she could have pulled away or stopped him with one word, but she didn't. Instead, her eyes slid shut as his mouth settled on hers.

She'd forgotten the feeling of being touched, of being kissed. Why had she waited so long in between? Then his arms slid around her and she forgot everything. All time and space stopped as he pressed his hard body next to hers. His hand was in her hair as her nails dug into his wide shoulders. Then his hand moved to her hip and pressed her closer to him and she let out a gasp as she felt his desire pressed close against her stomach.

Pulling back quickly, she took a step back. "I'm

sorry. I need to..." She looked around for any excuse, any reason to escape.

"Lauren?" He looked at her, questions in his dark eyes.

"No." She shook her head. "Don't. I don't... can't do this. I have too much on my mind right now." She started pacing while ticking things off on her fingers. "First and foremost is the ranch, will always be the ranch. I have fences to mend, a barn that needs repair, not to mention the house." She sighed and looked across the open field towards the old building. "So much needs to be done there. The roof leaks!" she blurted out and turned on him, feeling her head start to pound. "Then there's the cars. Don't get me started on the cars." She dropped her arms and shook her head, feeling defeated. "I'm sorry." She walked to the other side of Tanner and hopped up into the saddle in one quick movement. She'd forgotten about her incident with the barbed wire and when her backside hit the saddle, pain shot up her leg and she winced. "Do whatever you want. If you want to live in a dusty old rancher's house, move in. You'll get no argument from me. The one closest to the creek is open. But I expect you to honor our original agreement. No interference in the ranch, or with my life." She turned Tanner around and started back towards the house, then looked over her shoulder. "Oh, and Chase, if you mention our arrangement to anyone, you'll find yourself floating face down in the creek." She turned around and lightly kicked Tanner's sides, sending the horse trotting towards the house. She thought she heard Chase laughing, but didn't stop to look back.

When she got to the barn, she gently slid off the horse. The back of her leg was on fire, but she walked Tanner to his stall and took her time brushing him down. Then she made sure he and the other horses had plenty of water and fresh hay. It was supposed to be the ranch hands' job, but she enjoyed the simple task herself most days. Haley strolled in to the barn just when Lauren was done with the task. Her youngest sister always knew when the work was done.

"What happened to your pants?" Haley asked.

"I had a fight with the fence," Lauren mumbled. "Fence won. I'm going to go shower and clean up." She turned to walk out of the barn.

"I heard Chase Graham was here," Haley called after her. Lauren stopped and looked over her shoulder at her sister. Haley had a smile on her face, but upon seeing Lauren's glare, she quickly turned and went on her way, giggling.

The cool shower did wonders to clear her head. She knew things were changing around the ranch. You couldn't be a rancher if you didn't expect changes, but the fact that Chase was part of those changes drove her nuts. Why did it have to be him?

She remembered he'd always been at church and school events as a kid. In the summer months, he'd tag along with his dad to help out with the animals. She'd grown up seeing him and had been around him all of her life. It wasn't until the summer that she was eleven and he was twelve that she'd first felt her heart skip upon seeing him. He'd been helping his dad give all the new calves their shots. It had been a scorcher of a day and he'd removed his shirt, something she'd seen him do a hundred times. This time was different. This time he had man muscles all over. His skin had been tan and when he'd lifted a calf up to hold it steady, his arms had flexed and she'd lost her breath.

She wondered what that chest would look like now, then decided to dip her head under the cold water to clear the image her mind had conjured up. Why couldn't he have stayed away for a few more years? Just until she could get out from under his debt?

Later that evening, she and her sisters were out on the back deck grilling some steaks for dinner when her friend Savannah drove up in her Jeep and parked next to Lauren's truck. Savannah had been one of her best friends during grade school, but they'd grown apart when Savannah had started wearing makeup and chasing after boys. For her part, Lauren had been too busy helping raise her sisters and working on the ranch to deal with running boys.

Savannah had also become one of the largest

gossipers in town and, shortly after her parents had sold the oil rights to their land in middle school, she'd become spoiled rotten. She still lived in the mansion her family had built on their land, drove the newest cars, dated only wealthy boys, and wore only the best clothes. Lauren had fallen far down on her list of friends, but she didn't mind. She just didn't have the time to be the kind of friend that Savannah demanded.

Savannah got out and waved to them as she walked up the stone pathway in her three-inch heels. Her handbag probably cost as much as Lauren's truck. The diamonds in her ears sparkled when she flipped her long blonde hair over her shoulder.

"Oh, just what we need right now," Alex said under her breath.

"Hush! Be nice to our guest," Lauren whispered to her sister. Alex stuck out her tongue and crossed her arms over her chest just as Savannah walked onto the deck.

"Well, my goodness isn't this cozy." She walked over and hugged Lauren, making sure to kiss each of her cheeks.

"Do you want some ice tea?" Lauren hugged her back, holding the tongs away from Savannah's bright white blouse.

"Oh, that would be lovely." Savannah looked towards Alex, waiting.

"Alex, why don't you run inside and get our guest a glass of ice." Lauren glared at Alex until her sister stood and walked slowly into the house without a word.

"Have a seat, Savannah." She motioned towards the table, where there was a tall pitcher of tea and a bowl of salad. "Would you like to stay for dinner?"

"Oh, heavens, no. I don't eat meat anymore, remember?" Savannah sat in the chair and crossed her ankles. Lauren noted the small gold chain around her friend's ankle, not to mention that her friend's skirt was showing more leg then most of Lauren's swim suites did, but she kept her opinions to herself.

"That's right. I must have forgotten. How are your folks doing?"

Savannah looked bored. "Oh, they're the same. I was just out making runs trying to let everyone know about the charity ball we'll be holding at the end of next month at the Pine's Theater. It's for the animal shelter, just outside of town. I've always loved working with those poor creatures."

"Wow, that's wonderful of you." Lauren turned around and smiled at her friend. Ever since Savannah's family had come into money, they had started holding annual balls for one charity or another. Lauren thought it was a way for their family to rub it in the faces of everyone who had doubted them or criticized them for selling out to the large oil companies. The ball was less about raising funds for whatever cause they were trying to get behind and more about flaunting their wealth. But it always made for a good time and the town usually talked about it for months before and after the event.

Lauren remembered that Savannah had tried to work at the shelter once in high school. She'd gone a whole two days before getting fired. She couldn't keep a job for more than two weeks. Or a boyfriend, for that matter. Of course, she'd told everyone that she couldn't handle the smell of the place. "I'm sure it will be just as wonderful as last year's ball." Lauren walked over and sat at the table across from her and took a sip of her sweet tea.

Just then, Alex walked out carrying a large glass. When Lauren looked, her sister crossed her eyes behind Savannah's back. Savannah and Alex had never really gotten along. She supposed it all started in grade school when Lauren and Savannah had gotten into a little argument. The next day, Lauren had picked her sister to play with instead of Savannah. When Savannah had marched over and told Lauren she better play with her, Alex had stood up and told her that blood was thicker than friendship and that Lauren would always pick her over her friends.

Since that day, the two of them always kept their claws at bay, but let their tongues do all the lashing. Lauren had been caught in the middle of a cat war and, so far, she'd managed to keep the

"Yes, well. I'm determined to make it even better this year." Her friend's smile got really big. "I'm trying to get the Roy Carson Band. They're going to be in Tyler next month, and I'm just sure they'll be happy to play once they hear it's for a worthy cause."

"Wow, another ball," Alex piped in, earning a stern look from both Lauren and Haley, who had so far kept quiet. "I just can't wait." Alex's smile got really big, but her sarcasm didn't go unnoticed. Lauren kicked her sister under the table.

Savannah's smile didn't waver. "Speaking of animals, I hear Chase Graham is back in town. Didn't you two used to date?" She looked at Lauren who suddenly started choking on her tea. Finally, after she could breathe again, she shook her head.

"Date? No, Chase and I never really dated. We went out a few times, but you couldn't really call it dating."

"Oh, well." Savannah frowned a little. "I ran into him at the market this morning. That's why I decided to swing by and see you. I thought you ought to know." Then her smile was back. "He sure does know how to compliment a woman, doesn't he?" She fluffed her blonde hair. Savannah didn't believe in doing anything small. Her hair was what Alex always called Texas tall. Her shirt had so many sparkles on it, the sun flashed every time she moved. Not to mention the boulder-sized diamond earrings, necklace, and rings she wore. It was rumored that she'd had a breast enhancement in high school, although she'd already been blessed with D's at the time. Now they were the first thing most people noticed about her.

"Well, you are real pretty today in that outfit." Lauren hid the jealousy that had begun raging inside. If this was the kind of woman Chase liked, why was he kissing her in her field?

"Why, thank you. I just threw this on. Trying to drum up donations for the ball, I figured I might as well look pretty. Oh, I almost forgot." Savannah looked down at her manicured fingernails. "I was hoping you'd volunteer and help me out. I need someone to help sell tickets and I was hoping you'd talk Jamella into letting you put up a flier and sell some tickets at the diner." Savannah fanned herself.

"I'll ask. Do you—" she started.

"Wonderful!" Savannah reached into her purse and pulled out a stack of small folded fliers. "I was hoping you'd say 'yes.' Now, if you need more, I'd be happy to get you some."

Lauren looked down at the fliers. There was a picture of Savannah and her white Pekingese dog on the front wearing matching tiaras. Savannah prided herself on being the town's beauty queen. She always rode center stage in the town's parades and had on several occasions been named

Fairplay's Princess.

"Anyway, I better get back." She sighed and then stood. Lauren followed her to the edge of the deck.

"I'm so glad you stopped by." Lauren stood on the steps above her.

Savannah turned and hugged her. "Oh, me too. We simply must do lunch sometime."

"Sounds good. Drive safe." Lauren watched Savannah get in her white Jeep and drive away, slowly going over the dips and rivets in the long dirt drive.

"Thank god. Can you believe how much makeup she had on?" Alex leaned back and sighed.

Lauren turned and glared at her sister.

"No more than you wear on any date with Travis," Haley said. Alex glared at her little sister. Lauren started laughing and Haley followed. Soon after, Alex was joining in.

Chase stood in the market and looked down at the flowers. Which ones would Lauren like best? He knew he hadn't dealt with their last meeting the best way possible. He needed to show her that he didn't want to come in and take over everything. It had been a moment of craziness seven years ago when he'd proposed the crazy scheme of marriage for money. Okay, he'd had his reasons back then. His heart had led him to tie up his future in a tight little knot. He had wanted out of the small town for a while and was heading to college in Dallas. But he'd also known that he wanted Lauren. He just didn't know how to get everything. When he'd sat across from her that day seven years ago listening to his father and Mr. Holton talk to her about all the money she now owed them, he'd seen the despair in her eyes and he'd felt something shift inside.

He'd honestly just wanted to see that look go away. After the older men left, he'd sat out on the front porch swing and talked to her. He'd just suggested it in passing, not really meaning it, but she had looked at him with such excitement that he hadn't been able to turn back. The next day, unknown to everyone in the small town, they'd driven into Tyler and had signed the paperwork at the courthouse. Then he'd stopped by the bank that held the inheritance that had been left to him by his grandmother. He'd handed her the cash to pay her father's debt to his two best friends, and plenty for her to live on for the next few years.

A year later, while he'd been attending college in Dallas, he'd received a letter from her with a check. He'd thought about her message of wanting to pay him back, of wanting out of their arrangement, for two days before he'd sent the check back to her with a note saying he didn't want her money. Even then, he knew he didn't want out of their agreement.

He'd talked to Cheryl on the phone and had asked if Lauren was seeing anyone. When his father's assistant called him back a few days later, after confirming it herself, he'd been relieved to find out that Lauren was still single. If she didn't want free from their agreement because of personal reasons, he knew she just wanted to be free from him.

She'd tried again a few weeks later, this time sending money orders in his name. He'd returned those to her as well. Then six months later, she'd started sending him receipts from the local bank. The receipts showed both of their names on an account and the dollar amounts she was depositing.

One thing you had to say about her—once she had her mind set on something, she never gave up. Well, you could say that about him as well. He was determined to show Lauren that he was just what she needed. After seeing her for the first time in seven years, he realized how much he still wanted her. She'd done a lot of growing up since he'd last seen her; he supposed they'd both done some. He'd enjoyed exploring the new curves she'd developed since the last time he'd kissed her. Kissing her was like breathing again for the first time in seven years.

Now he looked down at the flowers. He set the white ones down and picked up the yellow ones. These reminded him more of her, so he walked up and paid for them, not noticing the looks the cashier gave him. As he drove out to the ranch, he thought about their meeting two days earlier.

His duffel bag and a small box full of his other effects were in his trunk. When he'd told his dad that he was moving out to her place, his father had just smiled.

"'Bout time," he'd said.

"I'm moving into one of the ranch houses, not the main house."

"Give it time, son." His father had laughed and slapped him on the back.

He drove to the ranch and turned off from the main drive, heading towards the farthest house on the dirt road. The smaller brick place looked like it had seen better days, but was still in pretty good shape. He dropped his stuff off, using the key hidden under the last porch step. The inside of the place looked new. All the appliances were well maintained, and the hardwood floor gleamed in the light. The furniture was simple yet comfortable. The small one-bedroom, one-bathroom place was all his for as long as he wanted. He knew Lauren had been telling the truth, that she wouldn't argue or ask him to leave.

After dropping off his stuff, he hopped back

into his truck and looked down at the flowers next to him. He hadn't planned on courting Lauren when he'd returned, but seeing her in the diner and being with her had made him realize that he still wanted her. After being gone for seven years, he still had a thing for her and now that he knew he was sticking around, he could pursue his feelings further.

When he drove up to her house, the first thing he looked at was the old roof. She'd mentioned that it leaked and he wondered why she hadn't had it replaced. He saw the spots where someone had tried to do some patchwork, but in his opinion, the whole thing needed to be replaced. The house itself could use a new coat of paint and some trim needed to be replaced. Then he noticed there were a few other trucks and cars parked over by the garage. Just how many vehicles did she have to run the ranch? He parked next to Lauren's truck, got out, and carried the flowers with him. Halfway to the back of the house, he heard her laughter coming from the barn and started walking in that direction instead.

When he walked into the barn, he blinked a few times to let his eyes adjust. Then he saw Lauren towards the back in the arms of another man, their silhouette highlighted by the brightness of the fields behind the opened doorway.

His fingers tightened around the flower stems and before he knew it, he was across the barn. He cleared his throat when he approached the couple.

"Oh." Lauren pulled back and looked over at him, and her smile fell away from her lips. "Hello, Chase." Her eyes went to the flowers he was holding by his side upside down.

The man dropped his hand off Lauren and took a step back. His face was shadowed by his Stetson hat, but when he moved, the light from the doorway hit his face. Chase stopped cold. "Grant? Is that you?"

Grant took a step forward and held out his hand. "Well, if this don't beat all. I heard you were back in town."

Chase was shocked. Grant Holton was a few years younger than him and had left town shortly after he had. Grant had been accepted into Harvard, which had at that time entered his name on Fairplay's biggest celebrity list.

The last time he'd seen Grant, he had been an overweight boy whose face was hidden behind large glasses. Now a tall, muscular man without glasses stood in front of him. He grabbed his hand and shook it fast. "I'll be damned." He looked over at Lauren. "Beg your pardon," he mumbled, and watched her smile. He turned back to Grant. "I hadn't heard you were back."

"Just got back yesterday. I was just getting a good look at one of Lauren's geldings here." He nodded to the horse that was standing in the stall beside them. "I've just bought the Wilkinson's place down the street and I'm in the market to get a horse." Grant smiled.

Chase didn't know if his friend was looking for anything else, so he took a step closer to Lauren, putting the question in his friend's eyes to rest. Grant looked down at the flowers and smiled. Then he took a step towards the horse, patting its mane when it stuck its head out the door.

He and Grant had been friends since the crib; their mother's had been best friends. Chase's mother had passed when he was younger. Grant's mother was still living and had taken it upon herself to help raise Chase after her best friend's death.

Chase and Grant started talking about Grant moving back to town, him buying a place and a horse. Both men had forgotten Lauren was standing next to them, until she cleared her throat.

"Are those for me?" She nodded towards the flowers he'd forgotten he was holding. He looked at them, smiled, then handed them to her.

"Just a little something to say I'm sorry about the fence-a-dent."

He watched as understanding flicked in her eyes then enjoyed the sound when she laughed. Her eyes sparkled in the dim light of the barn, and her smile lit up the darkness.

"Fence-a-dent?" Grant asked, his eyebrows shooting up.

Chase laughed. "Private joke."

"Well, if you two want to finish catching up, why don't you stay for dinner?" Lauren asked.

Grant shook his head. "I can't. I promised my ma I'd be home for dinner. She's pulling out all the fine china tonight. You might want to stop by and visit sometime. She'd be happy to see you." He looked at Chase.

"I sure will." They shook hands again.

"Well, I'll be by later this week with the trailer. He's just what I had in mind." He shook Lauren's hand and then bent down and placed a friendly kiss on her cheek.

"I know you'll be happy with him." She walked over and started rubbing the gelding's head. "Make sure to say hi to your folks for me."

"Will do." Grant nodded then turned and started walking out of the barn.

When they were finally alone, Chase walked over next to Lauren and started petting the gelding.

"Selling off this guy, huh?" The horse was trying to eat the flowers he'd just given to Lauren. She laughed and pulled them out of its reach.

"Yes, we took on a few younger ones last fall. Bob here is just too old to keep up with the young studs we have around here now."

"Bob?" He looked at her then laughed. "Still letting Alex name the animals, are you?"

"Occasionally." She smiled, then put the

flowers up to her nose and inhaled. "Still think you can buy me off with flowers, I see."

"Never underestimate the power of a good bouquet." He walked over to her. "Besides, I saw these and thought of you."

"That's because you know that daisies are my favorite." She smiled at him. "Remember the time we went picking them in the fields?" She sighed and looked out the door, then frowned. His gaze swept in the same direction and he saw Grant talking with Alexis outside.

Alex looked like she was about to eat the kid alive. "I'd better go break that up," Lauren said and started walking towards the doors.

He stopped her by putting his hand on her arm. "I think Alex can handle herself."

She looked at him with something close to humor in her eyes. "It's not my sister I'm worried about." She turned and waved her hand towards Alex and Grant. Now he could see what she meant. Alexis had on a pair of the shortest cutoff shorts he'd ever seen. Her tank top was tight and her bright red bra was showing a little around the top. Her hair was pulled up and she was wearing what could only be described as full war paint. Her eyes were painted a dark brown and her lips were deep red. He looked at Grant and realized the man did need saving. Grant's face was only a shade lighter than Alex's lips. Chase could hear him stuttering as he spoke to Alex.

"Yeah, we'd better go save him." He chuckled and followed Lauren out of the barn.

Jill Sanders

Chapter Four

Lauren pushed her feet and got the old rocker moving. Chase had left about an hour ago after having dinner with them on the back deck. She'd been so full of nerves, she hadn't really been able relax until now. She loved evenings like this. The stars lit up the night sky and the moonlight hit the fields, making them almost shine. She could hear the frogs and crickets chirping their hearts out. It sounded and felt like home. It had been almost a week since Chase had moved into the farthest house in the row of ranch-hand houses. Four of the small places had sat along the edge of the property since before she'd been born. After the tornado that claimed her mother's life, two of them had been remodeled.

Jimmy, her ranch foreman, lived in the largest

house, which was one of the remodeled ones. Larry, a seasoned ranch hand that had worked at the ranch since her father was alive, lived in one of the smaller places. Several seasonal men from Arizona were sharing the third place. Several additional men had trailers parked near the houses and would come and go each season. All in all, the men helped keep the ranch running smoothly.

It had taken her almost a year after her dad had passed away to get in the swing of running the huge place herself. Alex and Haley helped out with the horses and some of the chores around the place, but neither of them knew the extent of what she'd put herself through. She didn't want them to. She had hoped that they would go to college, but neither of them had shown any interest, though Haley was taking online classes. Lauren knew that neither of them had wanted to be a financial burden. Alex had actually started giving half her paycheck from the diner to Lauren to help pay the bills. At first, Lauren had declined to keep it, but after a week of arguing, she'd finally relented. Instead of using it around the ranch, as Alex had suggested, she'd opened a savings account and had put the money in it for her sisters to use someday.

Maybe Alex would use it for her wedding, something she'd thought about more often since Alex had been dating Travis on and off for the last few years. Lauren let out a sigh. It wasn't that she objected to Travis Nolan, Alex's on-again, off-again boyfriend…well, okay she did object to him.

She had always hoped her sister would do so much better. Travis was known as the bad boy in town. Not the kind that was a cool bad boy, but the kind that got into trouble all the time. His dad was the mayor of Fairplay and, therefore, Travis could do no harm. If he was pulled over for drinking and driving, his dad would be there to bail him out. Before the next morning, Travis's driving record would be spotless.

Lauren didn't know what Alex saw in the man, but she knew that her sister was going to do whatever she wanted. Haley had a boyfriend a while back, but after Wes had graduated from high school, he'd left town and gone on to basic training for the army. She didn't know if Haley had seen anyone since then, and to be honest, her sister wouldn't have told her if she had, since Haley was such an introvert. She hadn't always been like that. Before that fateful day when their mother was taken away, Lauren remembered Haley as being a chatterbox, someone who talked to anyone. Of course, she was so small back then, and she supposed most toddlers acted that way. Her sister was more comfortable around animals. At least that's how Lauren thought of her now.

She looked up at the night sky and thought of everything that had changed over the last seven years. She'd had her freedom and she owed it all to Chase. Why then was she having such a hard time with him being around? There had always been a pull of attraction between them. She would be lying if she said there wasn't. But something was different this time. It was almost as if she had no choice.

Pushing off from the old porch again, she set the old rocker in motion and decided that she was still in charge of her life. No matter who she owed or what decisions she'd made in the past, she was still Lauren West, daughter of Richard and Laura West. Her father and grandfather had built this place to be what it is, and she was even more determined than ever to keep it running and keep it in the family.

That next day started out like the rest. She woke up shortly before sunrise. But when she walked into the bathroom and turned on the shower, nothing happened. Then, to her horror, the pipes shook and loud noises came from deep within the old house, shaking the floors and walls just as black sludge started dripping from the shower head. Immediately she turned the knob, shutting it off. The pipes groaned and then all was quiet again. Walking over to the sink, she tried it with the same results.

Closing her eyes, she took a few calming breaths. In the last seven years, she'd had to play many roles around the large place: rancher, farmer, cook, maid, even mother to her sisters. But repairman was the worst hat she'd ever had to put on. Just two years ago, she'd had to replace some of the roof shingles after a large windstorm. She's painted, sanded, replaced light fixtures, and even once replaced a busted water pipe outside after a particularly cold winter. But she didn't even begin to understand why the water was doing what it was doing now. Wrapping her robe around her tightly, she walked to the downstairs bathroom and checked it. When the pipes groaned, she tried the kitchen.

Slamming her fist down on her thigh, she pulled on her father's old rubber boots, which always sat by the back door. Trudging out in the light rain, she made her way to the well house. Not that it was going to do her any good; she had no clue what she was looking for.

She knew hiring the local plumber wasn't in her budget this month. Actually, it wasn't in her budget for the next three months, not until they sold off the next lot of cattle in August. Opening the old gray well house door, she reached for the light switch and stopped cold. She'd been raised in Texas and knew the sound of a rattlesnake. Slowly she started moving backwards when she bumped into something solid. Hands came up and grabbed her shoulders to stop her from falling backwards.

"Stop!" She tried to push away, just as Chase pulled her back two feet.

"What the heck are you doing? Don't you know a rattler when you hear one? Are you trying to get yourself killed?" He pulled her away from the building a few more feet as the long snake stood its ground, just inside the open door.

"What do you think you're doing?" She put her hands on her hips and glared at him. What was he doing out here this early?

He pulled her back a few more steps away from the snake, which had decided the safety of the pump house was no longer for him. They both stopped and watch it slither off. When the snake was out of sight, she turned back to Chase and found him smiling at her.

"What?" She realized his arm was still on hers and that they were still standing a breath away from each other.

"I like the way you look in the morning." His smile got bigger. "You even smell nice."

She tried to pull away. "I doubt that, seeing as I haven't had a shower yet, since my water isn't working."

"What's wrong?" He started walking towards the small building. She fell in step with him.

"I'm sure it's nothing." She couldn't explain her desire to have him leave, but she didn't want his help on this. It was her place, her mess.

"I'll just take a look." He walked into the small building, flipping on the light and making sure there were no more snakes around. Then he walked behind the large water pump as she stood in the doorway. She knew what the pump was. It sat over their well, pumping and filtering their water, sending it to the house. She knew it was old.

She had to replace the filters on the thing two times a year, and since it was so old, she had to special order the filters from the local hardware store.

"Here's your problem." He walked back around the pump and motioned for her to follow him. She slowly walked around the large machine. Black ooze was slowly leaking from a broken pipe.

"I'm not a plumber, but it seems like your pump is dead."

"No! It can't be." She stared at the black ooze in full denial.

"Why wasn't this thing replaced years ago?" He turned off the knob leading to the house and turned to look at her.

"Because I didn't know it needed replacing." She stood there and felt like kicking the large hunk of metal.

"Taking one look in here, almost anyone would know it needed replacing. The thing is older than the hills." He shook his head.

She put her hands on her hips and glared at him. "It's not like I have a pile of money sitting around. I can't just go off and replace things that aren't broken."

"Well"—he stood back—"it's broken now. I'll talk to Billy when I go into town, see if he can get a new one up here later this week." Billy was the local plumber, the only plumber within thirty miles of town.

She felt the heat flood her face and knew the moment he spotted her temper rising. But she also knew that he probably was doing it all on purpose.

"How dare you! Just who do you think you are? I can take care of this place. It's mine, after all. If I need a new pump, I'll arrange for a new pump." She took a step forward and pointed her finger into his chest, pleased with herself when he took a step backwards and came up against the wall. "I don't want or need any help from you. I didn't ask you to come here." Her entire body was heated and vibrating with anger as she continued to berate him.

Chase stood there, his back against the wall as he listened to Lauren. Her face was flushed, her long hair was pulled up in a loose braid, and she was wearing an old blue flannel jacket over a thin robe, large black rubber boots, and hot pink pajama bottoms. He'd never seen her look better. He tried to focus on her words, but he just couldn't seem to take his eyes off her lips as they moved. Before he knew it, he'd pulled her into his arms and covered that sweet mouth of hers with his own. He had a few seconds before she started pushing him away. Using his hands, he gently cupped her face and kept her mouth to his until she stopped fighting all together. Her lips tasted like heaven; they were as soft as he'd remembered.

She leaned closer to him, putting her hands on his chest as a slight moan started in her chest, matching the one he felt rumble in his own. He felt her tilt her head and then her hands were in his hair, holding him closer.

Just then, the door to the small building flew open and Lauren jumped away from him so quickly, she almost fell backwards. He reached out and steadied her by holding onto her hips. Her hands went to his chest and they both looked over to the open door where Alex stood, smiling.

"Well, well, well." She leaned against the door frame. "I came out here to see what was wrong with the water. It appears like it all evaporated into steam with you two heating it up in here." Lauren's sister smiled at them. Chase couldn't help it, he smiled back and chuckled. Lauren glared at him, pushed him away, then straightened her clothes.

"The pump is broken. I'll go in and call Billy right now and see if he can come repair it." She turned to go, but Chase reached out and took her arm.

"It needs replacing." He watched her eyes heat.

"It will be repaired." He didn't let go of her arm.

"It needs to be hauled to the scrap yard. Lauren,

you need a new pump. There's no denying it."

She let out a large breath and looked at her sister.

"What?" Alex asked.

"Go on up to the house. I'll be there in a minute."

Her sister's eyes got big and she slowly crossed her arms over her chest. "I'm not some child you can boss around."

"Please, Alexis."

Alex looked between Chase and Lauren, then let out a large theatrical sigh. "Fine." She turned around and walked away, leaving the door wide open.

Lauren turned back to Chase and for a second he thought she was going to start yelling at him. Then she took a deep breath.

"Listen, Chase. I appreciate all that you've done for us in the past, but I've been running Saddleback Ranch for the last seven years. I know what needs to be done around here. If I say the water pump needs fixing, then that's what'll happen. I can't afford to replace it just yet and the repair will have to hold until I can."

"Lauren, you have a pile of money that's been sitting in the bank downtown for the past six years. And I know for a fact you haven't touched a dime of it to fix this place up." He held up his finger when she started to interrupt him. "This place is in dire need of some major repairs. So you can either own up to the fact that this thing"—he pointed to the large pump—"needs replacing or you can call Billy all the way out here and have him tell you it's beyond repair."

She crossed her arms over her chest and looked over at the old pump. She was silent for the longest time and he thought he could see tears building in her eyes.

"Fine. I'll go call him now." She turned and started walking out of the building, but then stopped in the doorway and looked back at him. The light behind her caused a halo to form around her dark hair, highlighting the honey richness hidden within the darker tresses. "I don't appreciate you interfering in the ranch. We had a deal, and unless you're going back on it, you'll stay out of my way." She turned and was gone before he could think of a reply.

She was right, after all. The twenty-year-old Chase had made a foolish deal. He'd been young and had desperately wanted something. Now, after seven years, he knew he didn't want to…no…he couldn't keep their original deal. He'd just have to amend some of the smaller points. He walked to the door and watched her stomp her way through the light rain to the back door of the old house.

It was true what he'd said. The place needed a lot of repair. Over the last six years, she'd chosen to put money into their joint checking account instead of doing what needed to be done to repair the old place. The white paint needed to be sandblasted and repainted. The whole roof needed repairing. Even the back deck was tilting to one side. He'd only seen the kitchen and dining rooms briefly last night when he'd been over for dinner, but he could tell the old stove was a fire hazard and the refrigerator looked like it was from the sixties. He doubted the upstairs had fared any better.

It had pissed him off seeing how she'd forced her family to live, choosing to be hardheaded about paying him back instead of using her money to live more comfortably. Hell, the small house he lived in at the edge of her property looked better cared for then her own place. At least she knew better than to let her employees live in shambles.

He pushed off from the door frame and walked a few feet in the direction the snake had gone. It wasn't normally his policy to kill an animal, but he knew the darn thing would find its way back to the cool building, and most likely next time he wouldn't be there to pull Lauren away to safety. It took less than two minutes before he heard the rattle and sliced the head off the large snake with the shovel he'd carried from the pump building. Digging a small hole, he tossed the body into it and covered it up. When he turned to put the shovel back, he noticed Lauren standing on the back deck, scowling at him. He reached up and tilted his cowboy hat and smiled the biggest smile he could. She glared at him and then turned to go back in the house.

All during his short drive into town, he thought about that kiss. He knew he wanted to kiss her again. He actually wanted to do more than just kiss her, but thought it would take a lot more kissing to soften her up before he could enjoy the feel of her body next to his. She was sure stubborn. He chuckled and remembered how she'd glared at him. He'd never had a woman glare at him like that before. Even when his mother had been alive and he'd gotten into trouble, she'd never glared at him like that.

Lauren would make a wonderful mother. His mind stopped and for a moment, his entire body went rigid. For the first time in his life, he was actually thinking about having kids. With Lauren. As he stopped at the one stop light in the middle of town, he looked over at the bank and realized what his next step was. He just prayed to God it wouldn't get him killed. He smiled as he parked his truck across from the bank and whistled as he walked across the street.

Jill Sanders

Chapter Five

Lauren walked across the street and tried not to feel let down. The sun was just rising and she had so much on her mind, she couldn't enjoy the bright colors flooding the sky. She had to pick up a few more hours at the diner just to cover the cost of Billy coming out to tell her the old pump had to be replaced. Now she was looking at having to use the profits from the sale of her old gelding to Grant to help pay for it. She knew that in the next few weeks she'd have to pick up any shifts she could at the diner to finish paying for the new pump.

When she walked in the front door, she groaned silently when she saw Chase and Grant sitting at the counter bar. Just what she needed, she thought. Walking behind the counter and through the swinging door towards the back, she dropped her purse under the counter, grabbed the coffee pot, and poured herself a cup.

"Morning, how's it going, hun?" Her boss, Jamella, walked around the corner with a tray full of food. She stopped for a second and looked at her. "You look like the cat drug you in this morning."

Lauren let out a quick laugh, wanting to break into tears. "Water pump is broken. Don't ask, right now. I'll be fine. I just need the extra hours. Thanks for letting me pick up today's shift." She spoke softly, hoping no one in the front heard her.

"Well, you can have as many as you want, since Barbara is out the next few weeks after her surgery." Jamella turned and walked out the swinging door to deliver a tray of food.

Lauren tried to postpone going out front for a few minutes. She just couldn't stand to see Chase and was hoping he'd leave before she walked out there. Of course, she wouldn't be so lucky.

"Hey there, Lauren." Grant smiled at her when she walked behind the counter. She avoided looking at Chase and smiled at Grant.

"Hi, there. How's Bob doing?" She started cleaning the counter top, not really thinking about the move as she pulled dirty dishes off and mopped up some spilled coffee.

"He's doing great. It took him a few days to get used to Mr. Tomas, my new Appalachian, but he's settled in just fine." Grant's smile got bigger. She smiled back. "Chase was just telling me he's living out at your place now." Her smile fell away and she felt her heartbeat in every vein in her body. Her eyes moved to Chase and she realized he was watching her very closely, a slight smile on his lips.

"The little place by the stream needs some fixing up. I was just enlisting Grant here to help me out."

She felt her heart slow and the red haze behind her eyes slowly disappeared. "If there's anything major, just let me know. I'll have Jimmy take a look." She saw Mrs. Roberts, one of the diner's regulars, waving from across the room. "Excuse me." She left the two men and walked over to the older woman.

"How are you today, Mrs. Roberts?" Lauren was happy for the reprieve.

"Oh, just fine today, Lauren. I heard you were having some work done out at your place today. I hope you aren't having too many issues with the old house."

Lauren smiled, knowing how fast word spread in small towns. She figured she'd have to explain herself a dozen times by the end of the day. "No, just some minor issues with the plumbing. Billy assured me that everything would be back up by the end of the day."

"Oh, that's good. I was worried when I saw all

those trucks heading out your way. Well, you will let me know if you need anything, won't you?" Mrs. Roberts smiled up at Lauren. Just then the bell chimed for the front door and Lauren looked over to see Mr. Graham and Mr. Holton walk in. The two had been her father's best friends, and since her father's death, their friendship had gotten even closer.

"Lauren, dear." The men walked over and took a seat in their favorite booth next to Mrs. Roberts. "We'll have our usual," Mr. Graham said as she walked over with a hot pot of coffee. Pouring each of the men a cup, she walked back to place their orders. Mrs. Robert's words hung in her mind like a broken record. Trucks? What trucks?

Four hours later, her mind was fried. She didn't know how Alex worked here thirty hours a week. She looked over at her sister and realized that, since she had arrived three hours ago, Alex's smile hadn't faltered once. Her makeup was still fresh, not a hair was out of place on her head, and she wore heels on top of it all. Lauren looked down at her black tennis shoes. Her feet were killing her and she desperately wished to soak them in a hot tub, which only reminded her that it might not be possible. A little more of her spirit slid to the floor.

Three more hours. You only have three more hours, she told herself. Then you can go home and sleep in your soft bed. She felt a bead of sweat drip down her back and cringed again at the thought of no shower when her shift was over. Instead, she knew she'd have to make do with a jug of water and a washcloth, like she'd used the last few days.

Growing up in East Texas, she knew that all it took in the summertime was a walk out to your car to be drenched in your own sweat, but spending seven hours on your feet, running around carrying hot plates and being around the hot kitchen, really did her in. She smelled like grease and coffee the second she stepped into the place.

If there was any other place to make a decent day's salary, she would have jumped at it years ago. By the end of her shift, she was completely worn out. Just looking at her sister and noticing how cheerful Alex still looked in the seat beside her made her feel even more down. How could she have so much energy? Alex had always been like that though. Maybe it was the fact that her sister didn't have the burden of the ranch's fate on her shoulders. At least she'd given her sisters that.

When they drove up the long driveway, her sister happily chatting about the day, Lauren looked at the house and hit the brakes, sending her sister jolting forward.

"What?" Alex gasped, "Are you okay? You're not having a heart attack are you?" Her sister quickly unbuckled her seat belt and reached for her.

"What? No!" She would have laughed, but her eyes were fixed on the house. "Look!" She pointed towards the large place. There across the field, with the sun setting behind it, stood her house with a shiny new metal roof on it. The new green sheets almost sparkled in the dying sunlight. The entire roof was done. How had someone done it all in one day? And without her notice? And who had done it?

Then her eyes squinted and instead of seeing green, she saw red. "Alex, you'll have to walk the rest of the way. I have to go kill someone." Alex looked over at her, her eyes still huge from seeing the new roof on the house.

"Lauren, I'm sure he didn't mean—"

"Out! Now." She playfully pushed her sister. "I'll deal with him and what he did or didn't mean myself."

Alex quickly gathered her bag up and stepped out of the car. "Lauren, I'm sure he was just trying to help. His father and our pa were best of friends. Don't really kill him, okay?" Her sister bit her lip, but smiled at her.

Lauren put the car in reverse without another word. She didn't trust herself to speak just then. She glanced at her sister in the rear mirror, then she drove as quickly as the little car would on the dirt road full of potholes.

When she reached the ranch house, she saw Chase out on the front porch leaning against the post with a smile on his face. He looked like he'd been expecting her. He wore a crisp white shirt tucked into his light colored jeans, and dark brown boots. His hat covered his eyes, but she was sure he was laughing at her.

She pulled the car to a quick stop, spitting up dust as the tires skid in the dry dirt. By the time she jumped out, she'd built it all up in her head and she knew there was no talking herself out of killing him.

"How dare you!" She slammed the car door and marched over to him, stopping less than a foot away from him. As she looked up the small step towards him, his smile got even bigger.

"Hello, Lauren. My, you are looking mighty pretty tonight." He tipped his hat up a little and she got a good look at his dark eyes. She was right, he was laughing at her. Pulling her arm back, she let it fly.

Chase wasn't really laughing at Lauren, more like he was laughing because he'd pulled it off. It had taken a crew of ten men, including himself, to get the new metal roof on. They'd finished the cleanup and the crew had driven away an hour before Lauren was going to be off her shift. He'd had time to get home, shower, and dress, and he'd just walked out on the front porch when he'd seen her car tossing up half the dust on the driveway.

Now he easily caught her fist and pulled her body close. Smiling down at her, he took a good look at her. Her hair was a mess, she had ketchup stains on her blue uniform, and she smelled like a greasy diner. Her eyes were wild and he could feel her temper vibrating through her.

Dipping his head, he placed a soft kiss on her lips and was shocked when she bit his lower lip. Pulling back, he laughed. "Lauren, you are a hellcat." He chuckled as he held her arms down as she tried to fight him. Then, when he had her arms safely tucked so he could avoid getting hit, he was rewarded with a swift foot to his shin. He was wearing boots and she had on a pair of tennis shoes, so she really didn't do any damage, but he pushed her back a step and held up his hands.

"Okay, okay. Give me a minute to explain." She blew a piece of her hair out of her face and glared at him.

"Explain? Explain how you crossed the line? How you went against our deal?" She crossed her arms over her chest and he watched her shirt tighten with the motion. Hell, he knew he was in trouble when she looked and smelled like she did and all he could think about was taking her inside and having her.

"Listen..." he began, only to be interrupted.

"You had no right. You broke your promise."

"Actually, if you think about it, you're the one who broke our deal. Six years ago, to be exact." He crossed his arms over his chest, matching her stance.

Her arms dropped away slowly and her chin dropped. "What? What are you talking about?"

He smiled and walked over to lean on the railing, then pointed to the small porch swing. She glared at him, but he just held his ground. Finally, she threw up her hands and walked over to sit down.

"Our original deal didn't mention anything about you paying me back." He crossed his arms.

She stood quickly. "Hold on." He interrupted her before she could yell further. "If you remember, I told you I'd give you the money, so you wouldn't have to pay my father and Mr. Holton back. In exchange, I wouldn't interfere with the running of the ranch. There was never any mention of paying me back. So when you started trying to send me checks, then opened the checking account and started making deposits, you broke our deal. She started to pace the small porch. "You broke our original deal. So I stopped by the bank the other day and pulled out some of that money you've been saving under our names and did what you should have done years ago—started fixing the place up, from the top down."

"You used my money." She stopped herself, shaking her head. "You used the money in your account to pay for my roof? Why?"

He stood up and took her shoulders and looked down into her eyes. "Lauren, you should have been using that money to fix the place up for the last six years. It needs so much work, it's almost falling down around you."

"I won't do this, Chase. I won't be indebted to you or your family." She pulled out of his grip. "I've taken care of my family, my property just fine up til now. I won't have you interfering again." Her eyes burned into his.

"I can't make you any promises." He leaned back against the railing and crossed his arms over his chest. He watched her eyes flash to his exposed arms and travel over his chest.

"Chase, stay out of my way." She looked up into his eyes and he saw her soften a little. Maybe she was trying a new tactic, because he saw her shoulders slump a little. "We don't need your help. I appreciate what you've done today, but please, keep your money." She turned to go. When she made it to her car, she looked back up at him. "I'll pay you back the cost of the roof as soon as I can."

Before the words had left her mouth, he was off the porch, pinning her to the side of her car. "Don't you dare. Don't you get it? I don't want your damn money. I never have and never will. You've been working yourself to the bone for that place, for your sisters. Letting it fall down around you isn't doing anyone any good. Use the damn money to fix it up. If you don't, then I will." He held her still and felt himself growling with anger. Didn't she get it? Maybe he hadn't shown her how he'd always felt for her. Maybe it was time.

Fueled on anger, he pushed his body up against her softness and took her lips in a searing kiss that spread heat to every muscle, every pore of his body. Her hands tried to push him off for just a moment, then she was pulling him closer, her fingers tangled in his hair. When she groaned, all his anger disappeared, replaced by lust so hot and powerful he almost lost control. When every muscle in her body had relaxed against his, he pulled back and watched as her eyes fluttered open slowly. Her lips were swollen, her cheeks were flushed, and her hair was still a mess. He smiled.

"Don't ask me to stop caring about what happens around here. I'm part of this place, part of you, whether you want me or not. I can help, I want to help."

"Why?" It was a whisper.

"You know why. You've always known why."

She shook her head, but he could see understanding in her eyes.

"Go." He took a step back. "Billy was able to install your water pump today. Go home, take a hot bath, think on it." He turned and walked up to the porch as she got in the car quickly. Before she shut the door, he looked at her and said, "Think of me."

Then he watched her drive back down the dirt road, slowly this time.

He stood out on the front porch until the crickets and frogs sang, then went inside and ate a cold sandwich and had one of the worst night's sleep he could remember.

The next morning he was in a sour mood, so when his father called and asked him to help out with his rounds, he jumped at the chance to deal with animals instead of humans for a day.

His first stop was to a little farm about an hour out of town. He'd known the old couple living there for as long as he could remember. He also remembered thinking they were old when he was in grade school. When he drove up, he was happily surprised to see that both of them still looked pretty spry. Martle stayed up on the porch, but waved as John walked out to greet him.

"Howdy, Boy!" John said, taking off his hat and wiping a little sweat from his brow. "Look at you, all grown up. It seems like just yesterday you were coming along with your pa, only standing this high." He motioned to just above his hips.

Chase walked forward and shook his hand. "You're both looking as young as ever." He smiled when the old man cussed, then quickly looked towards the porch like he was in trouble.

"Good thing Marty's hearing isn't what it used to be." He smiled and put his hat on his head.

"Well, come on back here. It's old Bessy that's been having problems." He motioned to the old barn.

When they walked into the coolness of the barn, Chase sighed. It had been a bitch roofing in the heat yesterday. Today was even hotter and the rest of the week promised to only get warmer. He'd been raised here and knew that summers could easily reach a hundred degrees a dozen or so times each year. Most the time he enjoyed it. Today, however, with only a few hours of restless sleep, it was just another annoyance.

By the time he had old Bessy fixed up with antibiotic pills and some ointment for a few cuts she'd received trying to break through a fence, it was lunchtime. He had three more stops after a quick sandwich from the cooler in the back of his truck, so that by the time he parked in front of his little house, he was covered in afterbirth from a few cattle that he'd been called out to help, and blood from a stray dog he'd found on the side of the highway. It had lost part of a hind leg and was now resting comfortably next to him in the cab of his truck. He carefully carried the small thing to the front porch and laid it down on an old rug. The terrier didn't budge, no doubt due to the meds he'd given it for pain.

Looking down at himself, he decided against tracking the mess into the house and shed most of his clothes right there on the front porch then walked the few feet towards the creek. The water wasn't very high now due to the heat, but he thought it would do the job of getting some of the slime off him before he took a proper shower inside. He dunked his head under and enjoyed the coolness of the creek, deciding to float and enjoy himself as long as he could. He was watching the clouds slowly drift by and the leaves stir overhead and must have fallen asleep, because he jolted straight out of the water when a rock splashed next to his head.

"What the…?" He looked across the water and glared at Lauren. She stood on the shore in the prettiest white summer dress he'd ever seen. Maybe it was because the sun was behind her, allowing him to see every curve underneath, or maybe it was because she had a smile on her face.

"Sorry." She smiled even more. "I did holler at you for a while, but you must have been too asleep to hear." Her eyes traveled over his bare chest. He felt like every last drop of water had just sizzled off his body and turned to steam under her gaze.

Chapter Six

"My, oh my," Lauren thought as she looked across the shallow water at an almost-naked Chase. It had been years since she'd seen him without a shirt. He'd gained a few more muscles since then and his skin was a wonderful shade of dark bronze at the moment. He must have worked on her roof without a shirt on. The irritation in his eyes changed to humor when he noticed her assessment of him.

She'd come over here today to apologize, since the cool bath last night had done wonders to clear her head. She'd been a jerk to him. He'd worked hard, along with half the men in town, to get her roof done in one day. Or so her sister Haley had told her when she had finally arrived home. At first she'd been mad that her sister hadn't called her and told her what was going on at the house, but after she explained that Chase had made her promise not to tell, she'd given up and understood she'd been outmaneuvered by a master.

He walked slowly out of the water like he was the master of the place. Lauren realized he'd always walked around like he was in charge. It was something she found quite entertaining and annoying at the same time.

Just then Dingo let out a quick bark. She hadn't wanted to bring the dog along, but when she'd opened the car door, the dog had jumped in and refused to get out. It was almost like she knew she was coming to visit Chase. Maybe it was the fried chicken in the basket that the dog had wanted?

Turning, she caught sight of a small bundle on his front porch. "Dingo, no." She set her basket down and started rushing towards her dog. "Leave it. Chase, something's crawled up on your porch to die." She approached the deck with caution.

"It's a stray I saved. Found him along Highway 69. Lost part of his back leg."

"Oh, you poor thing." She rushed to the porch and picked up the small creature who was just coming out of the drugged state.

"I wouldn't go doing..." It was too late. When she picked up the small bundle, it quickly opened its eyes and upchucked a little on her white dress. Chase groaned. "He has some pretty strong drugs in his system right now. He's likely to get sick for the next few hours."

She carefully set the dog back on the rug and watched as it whined. "You poor thing." She started to clean the front of her dress with a towel that had been hanging over the railing. She stopped when she saw him walking across the grass towards her, his wet boxers snug against his body. His legs were as impressive as the top part of him. He was smiling as he walked towards her, water dripping off every inch of his almost-naked body.

"Here, let me help you." He took the towel from her hands and started cleaning the front of her dress. She'd lost her ability to think, let alone be shocked at the fact that he was basically touching her breast. "Is that homemade fried chicken I smell?"

"Huh?" She couldn't take her eyes away from his dark ones. Actually, the more she looked into them, the more she realized they were a very warm shade of brown. She could see stardust speckles in them. It reminded her of a clear evening and watching the stars poking through the darkness of the night.

"Homemade chicken? In the basket?" He stopped cleaning her dress.

"Oh, yes. I made you dinner." She rushed over to where she'd set the basket full of food down. Dingo had sat next to the oversized basket, no doubt waiting for her cut of the meal. When she walked back onto the porch, he was walking out the front door with a pair of faded Levi's on. He'd yet to put on the white t-shirt he was carrying, and she desperately wished he wouldn't. His feet were still bare and he looked like he'd just come off the cover of a magazine she'd seen in the dentist's office once. He stretched up and slid on the shirt and her mouth went dry.

"Can you stay?" he asked when his head appeared from the shirt.

"What?" She shook her head to clear it. "Oh, sure. I suppose. I just wanted to thank you for yesterday. To apologize for my behavior. I'd had a long day."

"There's no need to apologize. I had one of those today. I know how they go. Would you like to sit out here or go inside?"

She looked around. The sun was sinking lower and the breeze had started bringing in cooler air. There was a large oak tree that sheltered half the house. An old picnic table sat halfway between the creek and the house, under another oak.

"How about we go sit under that tree and have a picnic."

"Sounds great. Do you want a beer?" He walked back to the screen door, waiting for her answer.

"Sure, I'll go set everything up." She walked to the table and busied herself. She loved cooking and picnics. Her sisters never really got into eating outside anymore unless it was on their deck. Some days she would take along a small basket on her rounds of the property. She'd find a cool tree to sit under and eat her lunch with Dingo and Tanner as company. She didn't mind, but it was nice to have friends to share meals with every now and then.

She took her time laying out the red and white checkered tablecloth, then set up the white plastic plates and forks. Taking out each Tupperware full of food, she arranged everything nicely. When she turned back around, Chase was there with a handful of white daisies he'd picked from the side of his house. His smile told her that he'd been watching her set the table. Looking down, she realized he'd pulled on a pair of boots and had a small cooler tucked under his arm, no doubt full of ice cold Shiner.

"You look beautiful." He handed her the flowers and she laughed.

"Well, aren't you the charmer." She smiled and pulled the flowers up to her face.

"You're the one that brought me fried chicken." He set the cooler down and pulled out two beers, opening one for her and handing it to her. She took a drink and let the cold liquid wet her dry throat. He opened his and took a deep drink.

"I needed this."

"The beer?" She sat down and smiled when he followed suit and sat across from her.

"No, although it doesn't hurt." He smiled and set it down and looked across at her. "I needed some good company. I needed to know that we were okay."

She shrugged her shoulders. "Of course we're okay. Why wouldn't we be?"

He mimicked her move by shrugging his shoulders. "I know you think I overstepped my boundaries."

"Don't. Let's not talk about it. Let's just eat and I'll be thankful I have a new roof and a new water pump." She smiled.

"Fair enough." He smiled over at her. They sat in silence for a few minutes, each filling a plate full of goodies she'd spent a few hours in the kitchen making.

She'd had plenty of time last night, since she couldn't sleep very well. Her mind kept running over his words, his actions from yesterday.

"You know why. You've always known why."

Did she know why? And more important, what was she going to do about it? She didn't want Chase to get the wrong impression with the food offering today. She wasn't condoning his actions, just trying to smooth things out between them. She still didn't want his help around the place. It was hers, and her sisters'. She still felt like she could have taken care of everything herself, given a little more time and a little more money.

The money she'd been adding into their joint account was going to be his, even if she had to sneak behind his back and get it to him. Two could play at this game and now that he had established that he wasn't going to play fair, her options were unlimited.

She smiled over at him and watched as he took a bite of the honey biscuits she'd baked earlier. "Grant was telling me that it would only take a few weeks to have our marriage annulled."

She watched his face go blank, then turn bright red as he started choking on the bite of biscuit. When his face turned a deep purple, she rushed over and started pounding on his back as he coughed. Finally, she handed him his beer and he took a large swallow followed by a few deep breathes. He startled her by standing up and grabbing hold of her shoulders.

"We are not getting an annulment," he growled out. His face had yet to return to its normal color, causing his eyes to stand out more.

"Why not? We haven't slept together. Besides, it's not like we're in love."

His hands dropped to his sides and he looked at her blankly. Slowly, his normal coloring seeped back into his face. Then he turned and sat down again. "We just aren't. It's the principle of it all."

"The principle?" She marched over and stood on the other side of the table. "The principle? Are you telling me that there is no way we are ever going to stop this joke? It's gone on long enough, don't you think?"

"Joke?" He took another drink of his beer and looked at her, humor flooding his expression and eyes.

She started pacing, waving her hands around as she babbled and explained what she'd practiced saying to him all last night and this morning as she'd cooked.

"Sure, this is a joke. I mean, who goes and gets married all because of a loan between two friends. I mean, this is so seventeenth century. It's not like we had an arranged marriage." She turned and glared at him when he chuckled. "It's beyond my comprehension why you insisted on it in the first place." She started walking below the low branches of the tree again, back and forth. "I was too emotional after losing my father to think clearly. There I was, my father gone, the weight of the ranch on my shoulders, along with my responsibility for my sisters, and then the new debt I owed your father and Mr. Holton. You waltzed in with an offer to remove all it. All I had to do was sign on the dotted line. Of a marriage license." She turned to him again. "You took advantage of me." He'd continued eating while she ranted, but upon hearing her last words, he slowly placed his hands on the table and stood up. His eyes heated.

"Lauren, you're playing with fire."

She looked at him and knew that she'd crossed the line. He hadn't taken advantage of her. There were so many other ways he could have, but he hadn't. He'd been a total gentlemen about the whole thing. A friend. That's all he'd been. She'd just always assumed that once she'd paid him back in full, that they would quietly get a divorce.

But the other day, when Grant had been over, she'd mentioned a friend of hers who'd entered into a marriage and wanted out. He'd told her all about annulments and filled her in on what it would take to have her friend get one. She had a new goal instead of divorce, now.

"Are you telling me that I'm stuck with you?" She put her hands on her hips, waiting for his answer.

He just looked back at her with a blank face, then slowly a smile crossed his lips. "Yeah, I guess I am." He turned and sat back down, picked up a chicken leg and bit into it.

She couldn't believe her ears. Did he honestly think she'd stay married to him? She didn't have any immediate plans to marry someone else, but she'd always thought it would happen in the future. Someday she'd find someone she'd want to settle down with. He'd have to want to live and work on the ranch, be liked by her sisters, and most importantly, not be Chase Graham.

She turned and, without a word, left him sitting under the old oak, eating her food. When she opened her car door, Dingo jumped in. "Yeah, I'm done here, too." She slammed the door a little louder than normal. Chase looked up and waved as she drove off, a huge smile on his face.

"Can you believe he won't give me a divorce?" She looked over at Dingo. The dog hung her head out the window and enjoyed the breeze. "We will just see about that."

Chase's laughter dropped away as soon as Lauren drove away. Great! Just what he hadn't wanted to talk about today. He'd been happily surprised that she'd brought him food. She'd gotten him out of the mood he'd been in earlier. Now, as he looked over at her untouched plate, he wondered why she was being so difficult? Couldn't she see that the best solution for them both was this marriage? He looked up and saw the little terrier hobbling towards him. The dog was moving slowly, but looked like he was getting the hang of walking on three legs instead of four. When he made it to the table, he sat down. "You'll get the hang of it, buddy." Chase tossed him a whole biscuit, knowing the bread would help soak up some of the acid in its small stomach.

By the time he was full and had cleaned up their

little picnic, Chase was feeling guilty. He supposed he should have talked to her a long time ago about his plans, but he'd had his reasons not to.

Stuffing all the food back into the large basket, he carried it and the small dog back to the front porch. The dog curled up on the rug again as he carried the basket into the house. Putting the leftover food away, he decided a trip to his dad's might cheer him up.

When he and Buddy got there a half hour later, his shirt was dirty thanks to Buddy deciding to upchuck the biscuit all over him. He didn't mind; in fact, he was used to getting animal fluids on him. It was better than getting bit or kicked, which he'd had plenty of as well.

When he walked up to the porch carrying the small dog, his father opened the door before he could knock.

"What have you got there?" His father reached out and took the small thing from him. "Poor guy. Come on in. You too, son."

Two hours later, he and Buddy left his dad's place, both with smiles on their faces. Buddy, for his part, had started feeling well enough to play with his dad's old Irish setter. The pair had quickly become best friends, and Chase had made up his mind to keep the three-legged dog. It was about time he settled down with a dog of his own. After all, people tended to trust a vet who had his own animals. At least that's what his father had told him several times during his visit.

By the time he drove up to the ranch house, he was exhausted. The last thing he needed was to see Lauren's sister standing on his porch with her arms crossed over her chest like she'd been waiting for him.

He got out of the car, carrying Buddy in his arms.

"What have you got there?" Alex stood on the deck and opened her arms. "Oh, you poor thing." She snuggled with the small dog, then looked up at him. "And to think I'd come over here to tell you what a heartless slime you are."

He laughed a little. "What did I do now?"

Alex walked over and sat down in the chair so she could enjoy the small dog. "I don't know. But whatever it is, you sure have Lauren in a mood. She's actually cleaning the house."

He sat next to her. "That can't be that much of a shock. I've seen your place, and it's pretty clean." Alex was Lauren's opposite. Where Lauren had long rich chestnut hair and sexy green eyes, Alexis had blonde hair and deep brown eyes. He'd been told that she looked a lot like their mother had, whereas Lauren and Haley took after their dad's side of the family.

"She's not just cleaning downstairs, but the whole house. The attic, too. We haven't stepped foot in there since dad passed." She set the dog down when he started whining. Buddy went and jumped off the porch and walked over to the nearest tree and lifted his bad leg to relieve himself. Alex looked over at Chase. He couldn't see what was going on in her dark eyes, but he could tell she was trying to figure out her next move.

"I like you, Chase. I've always liked your family, but if you cross my sister in any way, I'll have to kill you." She said it with such enthusiasm, he had to laugh.

"I like you, too. And your family. What's going on between me and your sister is private, but I appreciate you coming out here and having this talk with me. I'd do the same to anyone who messed around with someone in my family."

"Fair enough. You've been warned. I also came by to say thank you for the roof. I know it was you who paid for it, don't ask me how. So, I have something for you." She walked over to her car and leaned in the open window and pulled out a pie plate. "It was our ma's recipe." She handed it to him. He peeled back the tin foil and the smell of apples and cinnamon hit him.

"Yum, my favorite."

"Who doesn't love apple pie?" She smiled at him, then her smile fell away. "Thanks again. I don't know what you get out of it, but Haley and I wanted to say thank you. Okay, Haley baked the pie, but I'm delivering it." She smiled again. She headed back to her car, but stopped before getting in. "Chase, I don't mind you sticking your nose in some places, but Lauren, well...She's different. She likes controlling things. We sort of let her, but it's nice to know that someone else is out there looking out for her. By the way, she'll be riding fences again this weekend. She plans on heading up to the hills, camping out all by herself with just her horse and the dog to keep her company. Haley and I hate it when she does that." Alex frowned. "On a lighter side, if you ever want to just go for a ride, Buster's available for you. He's a big guy, but gentle enough. You're welcome to take him out whenever you want." A small smile crept onto her lips and Chase laughed.

"Your message is received loud and clear. Tell Haley that if she could watch Buddy, here"—he nodded towards the small dog who was lying down at his feet now—"this weekend, I'd appreciate it. He's not up to going on rides, short or long, yet."

She nodded her head and smiled. "Thanks. See you around."

Chapter Seven

Lauren was off to an early start on Friday. She lived for weekends where she could take Tanner and Dingo up in the hills and disappear for a while. She had a few stops around the fields first, but by ten, they were on their way up the hills. Dingo jogged along for a while, then started whining. Lauren stopped Tanner and Dingo jumped up into her lap, using her boot as a step. It was a trick she'd taught the dog when she was younger, and it had paid off.

Her property was rich in grassy hills. The farther she went into them, the thicker the pines and brush got. There were about five hundred acres that lay between the house and the next development. If you chose the right pathways, you could go weeks without crossing roads or coming upon another ranch house. Lauren knew all the pathways to take for her weekend trip. Her saddlebag was packed with everything she'd need. Her cell phone was turned off and tucked into a pocket on her bag, just in case. She had her shotgun and her pistol, and a box of bullets for each within easy reach, something her Dad had taught her to do. You never knew when a wild boar would jump out at you or a snake would cross your path.

Thinking of snakes, she remembered the morning at the pump house with Chase, which got her thinking about water and seeing him near naked with water glistening off his chest and arms.

She shook her head clear of images of Chase. This was her time away from him, away from everything. There was no way she was going to think of Chase or what he did to her any more this weekend. This weekend she wanted to be selfish. She turned down the path that would lead her up to an old cabin her dad had built before she was born. She liked to stay at it during her weekend trips. She had to duck for a large branch that Tanner had walked under, and was surprised to hear a horse and rider behind her. Thinking it was one of her sisters, she looked over her shoulder and pulled Tanner to a stop to wait. Sometimes Haley liked to ride the trails. Hopefully, whoever it was wasn't coming along for the weekend.

When she saw Buster's head pop around a tree branch, she smiled and called out to her sister Alex.

"Alex, are you just..." Her words fell away as the rider came into view. Chase smiled at her from Buster's back. His long legs hung over the horse's large girth. His boots sat in the stirrups and he looked very comfortable in the saddle. He wore a light tan jacket and a Stetson that matched.

"Oh." She tried to think of something to say. Just then, Dingo let out a happy bark. The dog always seemed to be late in warning her when it came to Chase.

"I hope you don't mind. We were just out for a ride. Alex said it would be okay if I took the old guy out for a while." He sat forward and patted Buster's head.

Tanner gave a snort of welcome to his old friend who returned the greeting. Then the two horses quieted down again and Lauren was left not knowing what to say. She saw that his saddle was packed with a large bag, most likely full of items for a longer trip.

"Are you camping?" She squinted her eyes and looked at him cautiously as Dingo tried to jump into Chase's arms.

He patted his bag and smiled bigger, then caught Dingo as she landed softly in his lap. "I was thinking about it. I haven't taken any time to myself since I returned to town. If it's alright, I'll just tag along with you."

"Did Alexis put you up to this? I know they

don't like me going out by myself, but to ask you along..."

He held up his hand. "Whoa, no one forced me to come along. Honest, I just needed to get away for a while. I saw you back at the base of the trail and thought I'd follow you, since you know the area a lot better than I do. That is if you think you can stand my company."

She knew he was just pushing her buttons, but she straightened her back and threw her chin up a little, taking the challenge. "Of course I can. If you can keep up with me, you're welcome to tag along." She turned Tanner around and started back up the trail, trying not to let his laughter get on her nerves too much.

They rode in silence for almost an hour, enjoying the cool breeze blowing between the trees. Lauren always loved this part of the year. Even though she had to keep a can of bug spray on her, she didn't mind the heat and humidity. Of course, it meant that she had to stop and water the horse more often. When she made it to a clearing that had a small stream flowing through a green field, she stopped Tanner and looked behind to see Buster and Chase right behind her. Dingo lay comfortably in his lap, like she belonged there. She'd hoped that he'd fallen behind a little, or had decided to turn down a different path, but there he was, looking like he was enjoying the ride.

"We'll stop and water the horses and grab some

lunch. Did you bring food? Because I only brought enough for one."

He smiled and nodded. "I'm all set."

She felt a little deflated, hoping he would have a reason to turn back. She watched as he smoothly tossed his leg over the horse and slid off in one quick motion. He set Dingo down and she quickly raced to the water's edge and start lapping up a drink. Then Chase walked over and took her hips and pulled her off Tanner.

"I can get off my..." Before she could finish, he was kissing her. His mouth was hot on hers, taking what he wanted. Her back was up against Tanner's side and Chase's hands were gripping her hips, pulling her closer to him until she felt all the wind knocked out of her. Then as quickly as he'd started, he pulled away, leaving her leaning on her horse and trying to catch her breath as he turned to grab Buster's reins.

It took almost a minute for her mind to click into gear again. Then she grabbed up Tanner's reins and walked over to where Chase had tied the other horse to a low branch so he could drink from the small brook. She threw Tanner's reins over the branch and watched as her horse started enjoying the cool water, then she turned on Chase.

"What the hell was that? Do you think you can just come up here and manhandle me?" She pointed her finger into his chest and glared at him. "I've got news for you buddy, I'm not..."

Again, he stopped her by pulling her close. She saw the smile on his face before his lips claimed hers again. This time she was prepared. Her booted foot came up and connected with his shin. His boots protected him from most of the impact, but he still grunted and pulled away.

"Damn it, Lauren." She watched as he jumped up and down on one leg. His hat had fallen off and had landed in the dirt. He looked so funny jumping around like that, she couldn't help it, she started to laugh. When he looked over at her, a frown on his face, she laughed harder. The horses even stopped drinking water and looked over at her.

It might have been all the stress finally getting to her, but she just couldn't stop herself from laughing. Finally, she sat down on the bank of the brook next to where she'd dropped her bag and held her sides. Chase hobbled over and grabbed his bag off Buster's saddle, then sat down next to her in the short grass, rubbing his shin. Dingo ran around in the field behind them, enjoying the freedom.

"Feel better?" His smile was a little crooked. His eyes were scanning her, like he was trying to gauge her emotions.

Smiling over at him, she nodded. "I guess I needed that. Thanks."

"Anytime." He rubbed his shin while keeping his eyes on her. Then he chuckled and she felt warmth spread throughout her body.

Taking her eyes off his, she opened her bag and pulled out a sandwich and a bottled water and focused on her lunch. After a few bites, she started talking about everything and anything. She hadn't felt nervous around him since...well...ever, but now for some reason she couldn't stop herself from talking.

"I was heading to my dad's cabin." She waited for his approval. He nodded and she continued. "If you want to tag along, we should be there around nightfall. I always love staying there in the summer. The place just feels right when I need some time away. Living with my two sisters has its ups and downs." She smiled over at him. "You're lucky that you never had any siblings." Then her smile fell away when she remembered that his mother had died while giving birth to his stillborn sister. "I'm sorry." She took another bite of her sandwich to shut herself up.

"It's okay." He took a drink of his own water. "I would have loved having a younger sister. I can only vaguely remember my mother. I remember laying my head on her large belly, listening to Jessie's heartbeat. That's what they were going to name my sister. Actually, they didn't know it was a girl at that point." He chuckled a little. "My father told my mother it was a girl and he wouldn't hear anything else, so my mother said Jessie could be a boy's name, too." He sighed and looked off across the small creek and field. "I envy you your family. I know we both lost our mother's around the same time, different circumstances, but you have your sisters. Being raised alone has its moments, but I always dreamed of having siblings like you do." He looked over at her, his eyes searching hers.

"I guess I've never thought about not having my sisters around. They do make life...interesting." She smiled as she looked off to the far side of the field. She was surprised to see a medium-sized doe nibbling on the grass near the edge of the trees. Nodding her head, she smiled. "Look." She pointed towards the deer and watched as he looked, then smiled as he spotted it. "In a few more months she'll be hiding from the hunters. But for now, she's enjoying the sun and the tall grass." Lauren took a deep breath and lay back in the grass, folding her arms behind her head as she watched the clouds slowly drift by in the blue sky.

Chase finished his sandwich and then lay down next to her. "Why is it so important for you to do everything on your own?" She turned her head a little and looked at him. He turned onto his side, his left arm supporting his head as he propped up on his elbow and looked down at her.

"I don't like to be dependent on others. My father was and he worked himself to death trying to pay back the loan he took." She looked off to the sky again. "I don't want to be like that. I want to answer to no one. If something at the ranch needs fixing, I want to be able to have the money to do it. I just need another year and I'll be at that place. The ranch pays for itself. Actually, with the sale of the cattle this fall, I'll be able to pay you off completely. Then I can do whatever I want." She smiled and closed her eyes for just a moment.

Chase looked down at her dark eyelashes. Her hair was spread out on the green grass on the bank of the stream, blowing lightly in the breeze. Her cheeks were flushed from the ride and the heat of the day. Her tan shirt was a little dusty from the trail. She'd unbuttoned the top three buttons so he could see the dip on her throat and instantly thought of what it would taste like.

"You don't have to pay me back. I don't want or need your money." It was an old argument, one he knew he'd probably never win.

"I know. I need to do it for myself. I need to know that I can." She opened her eyes and looked up at him. He'd moved closer to her, so that he was hovering just above her. He saw her eyes go wide, then she recovered and put her hand on his shoulder. "Chase, please don't." It was just a whisper.

"Why? Why can't you take a moment to enjoy things? Why can't we just enjoy what's between us?" He leaned closer. "You're not afraid of me, are you?" He smiled slightly, enjoying the challenge he saw in her eyes just before she reached up, took his hair, and pulled him down to her lips.

He couldn't explain the zing he felt when she touched him, when her soft lips touched his. She let out a low moan, and he rolled until she was lying next to him and their legs were tangled. Her hands were fisted in his hair as his fingers roamed over her hips, pulling her closer, exploring every inch he could.

As he reached up and put his hands on her face, he gently pulled her head back so he could feast on her neck. He nibbled the sweet column until he reached the top of her blouse, then with shaky fingers he unbuttoned the next small buttons until he could see a white silk tank top. Once he had her blouse open, he leaned back and looked at her. The silk was bunched up, so that her flat belly was exposed. He slowly ran a finger down her neck, over her shoulder, lower, until he reached the exposed skin. He watched her arch her back and could tell she wanted more. Leaning over, he placed a soft kiss on her belly button and heard her catch her breath.

"More?" He trailed his finger over the edge of her jeans and watched her hips jolt. His eyes flew to hers. She was watching him, her green eyes the color of the grass below her. He lost his breath at how beautiful she was. His hand stilled as her hand reached up and touched his face, then she was pulling him back down, and he was a slave to her every command.

She rolled him over until she straddled him, then in a quick motion, she discarded her shirt, leaving her with just the white see-through silk above. Her skin looked so soft, he just had to reach up and touch her hips as she started unbuttoning his shirt. A nervous laugh escaped her lips as she fumbled with the last button. Finally, she tried to pull his shirt off his shoulders. He had to sit up a little so she could finally pull it free. He had a white tank top on underneath, but she was satisfied with shyly running her fingers over his forearms. He leaned up and started kissing her shoulders; the way the sun was hitting them, he had to have a taste. She tasted as good as he'd imagined. She smelled of something sweet and tasted even better. He slowly moved his hands up her hips until he ran his fingers just under the silk and touched her sensitive skin. Her head fell back, and her dark hair flowed over her shoulders and gleamed in the sunlight. Using his tongue, he wet the silk over the dark circles he'd seen, using the wet silk to please her until her nipples puckered for his exploration.

Her fists clung to his hair and her hips started to move against his. He swore that if he made it out alive, he'd do all he could to make sure she knew how much he'd wanted this, wanted her.

Just then a shot rang out a dozen yards from them. The horses jolted, pulling on their reins until the small branch they'd been tied to threatened to break loose. Chase jumped up and grabbed their reins before they could bolt. Dingo let out a few low growls, then began to bark towards the trees. When Chase looked over, Lauren had her shirt in one hand and a pistol in the other.

"Where were you hiding that?" he asked, while trying to calm the horses.

"Someone's shooting on my land. Probably after that doe we just saw." She was scanning the tree line as she yanked on her shirt, tucking it in with quick, jerking motions. "Stay," she told Dingo, who looked like she wanted to bolt into the trees. Lauren walked over, tucked the gun back into her boot, and grabbed for Tanner's reins.

"Oh, no you don't." He held them up, away from her. "If you think that you're chasing after some illegal hunters, you'd better think again. Besides, it was probably one of the ranch hands. Aren't they usually around here?"

She shook her head. "Jimmy's got them all fixing the fence on the east ridge. They'll be at it all weekend. That's someone hunting on my land, illegally, and I have the right to make sure they—"

"Lauren." He stopped her. "Let me make myself perfectly clear. Illegal hunters don't think twice about bending the law. They don't care whose land they are on or what season it is. And"—he emphasized his next words—"they don't hesitate to remove any obstacle. No matter how pretty she may be. You are *not* getting on this horse to hunt down some hunters."

She stood there, her arms crossed over her pretty chest, her eyes flaring with anger. "Fine." She walked over to retrieve her bag and jacket from the water's edge. "They're probably long gone by now, anyway." She shook off her jacket and put it on. "We'd better get going if we're going to make the cabin by nightfall."

When he had gathered his stuff, she expertly mounted her horse then watched him jump onto Buster's back.

By early dusk they had reached the small clearing and the cabin came into view. Its tin roof shined in the fading light.

"It doesn't look like much, but it's home away from home." Lauren was smiling as they moved closer to the old building. Then she frowned and furrowed her brow and she looked towards the cabin.

"What?" He looked back at the building and could see that the door stood wide open. "Stay here." He turned his horse and stopped her from moving forward. Dingo started growling, and the hair on the back of Lauren's neck stood up. Lauren told the dog to stay as Chase slowly removed his shotgun from the holder. He always brought it with him when he went into the woods. He'd been raised in the country and knew it was invaluable to ensure your safety, especially since there were a lot of wild boars in the area. "I mean it Lauren. Stay put. Promise me."

She nodded her head. He turned the horse around and went a few more yards. Then he tied Buster up to a tree and started walking towards the building, slowly. He didn't see any vehicles or horses and doubted whoever had broken in was still around. When he got closer, he saw some four-wheeler tracks. It appeared that whoever had been staying there had had fun peeling out in the muddy fields. They'd most likely been there in the early spring, since the mud was now dry and flaky from the summer heat.

Still, he approached the cabin carefully. When he got to the porch, he noticed the lock had been shot off. There was a hole in the door where the padlock used to be. He used the barrel of his shotgun to open the door the rest of the way. It was dark in the cabin and it took a minute for his eyes to adjust. Pulling out the flashlight he'd brought along, he flipped it on and almost shot a pair of raccoons as they jumped from a table full of empty food cans. He moved aside so they could scurry out the door as fast as their fat bodies would go. Dingo gave chase. Laughing, Chase turned around and saw that Lauren had not obeyed him. She stood two feet away, smiling at the raccoons.

"Well, so much for catching the bandits." She laughed.

"I thought I told you to..." He dropped off. Why waste his breath? He knew she wasn't going to listen to him. Shaking his head, he walked back over to his horse. "Looks like we'll have to clean the place up a little. Squatters never clean up after themselves."

"Oh!" She gasped and he spun around, his gun ready. "Can you believe they stole the generator? I was looking forward to reading tonight." She stomped her boot.

He could see the spot on the front porch where a large generator once sat. The electric cables to the house had been cut clean.

"Looks like you'll just have to rough it." He turned back to the horses and gathered both of their bags.

"Hopefully they didn't steal all the candles," she said as she walked into the small building.

When he walked back in, she had a few candles set up so that there was enough dim light that he could see it was a one-room cabin. Four small cots were lined up against the back wall, close to an old iron stove.

Looking around the space, he started questioning his decision to come along. It was going to be pure torture sleeping in the small space with Lauren right next to him.

Jill Sanders

Chapter Eight

$\mathcal{L}$auren tossed and turned for the hundredth time. How was she expected to sleep with Chase just a few feet away? Especially after what they'd done at lunch. Her mind had wandered so much that she couldn't even remember the rest of the trip to the cabin.

They'd sat across from each other at the small table last night eating dinner and she hadn't known what to say. So she'd talked about the cabin and about some of the great times she and her sisters and their father had had there. He'd laughed when she'd told him about Alex almost falling into the outhouse and how she had never returned to the cabin since that day, over ten years ago.

After they'd eaten, Lauren yawned, which led to an awkward attempt to change clothes. Chase had ended up excusing himself and had gone outside while she'd quickly changed and crawled into her sleeping bag. She'd pretended to be asleep when he'd returned half an hour later.

She didn't know why she was such a coward around him. Maybe it was because she wasn't experienced in these matters? Did he know that she'd never been with anyone like that before? Could he tell? It wasn't as if she'd purposely avoided being with someone. She'd just never found someone she wanted to be with. She'd had a few dates in high school, but for the most part, she'd been too busy with the ranch when she wasn't at school to deal with boyfriends. Then, after her father had died, she'd felt honor-bound not to get involved with anyone. She didn't view her and Chase's marriage as real, but she still took their wedding vows seriously. She was no cheater. It wasn't as if it had been a hardship. She'd had little interest in anyone in town and even less time to pursue a relationship, even if she'd wanted to.

Morning came sooner then she'd hoped. It had taken her half the night to finally get comfortable enough to fall into a light sleep. She'd planned on waking before Chase did, but when she opened her eyes, his bunk was already empty.

Quickly getting dressed, she rinsed her mouth out with a bottle of water and some toothpaste. She was braiding her hair when Chase and Dingo walked in. Chase had a handful of wildflowers in his hand.

"Thought you'd want to sleep in a little after that rough night of sleep." He smiled quickly. She glared at the flowers.

"What are those for?" She took the flowers when he handed them to her and smelled the sweet scents.

"Does a man need a reason to give his wife flowers?"

He leaned back on his heels, watching her. Her eyes bore into him. "I'm not your wife." He smiled quickly and tilted his head.

"Well, technically...You know what I mean." She walked to the door and opened it, needing the fresh air.

"I started breakfast." He came up behind her and laid a hand on her waist, turning her towards him. "Lauren." He placed a finger under her chin and turned her head until she looked into his deep eyes. "I like the way it sounds, calling you wife." He smiled a little and she pulled back.

"Don't start." She tried to pull away, but he just held her closer.

"I couldn't sleep all night from wanting you." His finger went from her chin, slowly down the column of her neck and she felt herself shiver in the warmth of the summer morning.

She had too much riding on this; she couldn't afford to get distracted. "Chase, I can't."

"Yes, you can." He smiled just before he leaned down and set his mouth on hers. Heat spread throughout her entire body, causing her skin to feel like it was steaming. How did he do this to her each time? She just couldn't think clearly with him touching her, with him kissing her like he was now, using his tongue and teeth to send ripples of desire so strong down every nerve in her body. Her arms wrapped around him on their own accord and her fingers tangled in his thick hair, holding his mouth to hers.

She was breathless when he pulled away and placed a hand over her shoulder, holding himself up with the door frame. He rested his forehead against hers and closed his eyes. "There is something here that I've never had before, and I'll be damned if I'll just walk away from it." He opened his eyes and looked deeply into hers. "You feel it, too. I can see it." He waited until she finally nodded her head. He was right. She couldn't deny what was so obviously written on her face. "Stop fighting it then and let's see where this leads us." He pulled back and brushed a strand of loose hair away from her eyes.

He was right. There was no reason, other than fear, to keep backing away.

"Chase?" She reached up and took his face in her hands.

"Yes?" He smiled down at her.

"You're burning our breakfast." She smiled at him, then ducked under his arm and walked over to the fire pit. He rushed over and, using a small towel, pushed the pan off the fire while she laughed.

After eating their slightly burnt oatmeal and toast, they set off to the far side of the ranch where her property ended. They rode the fence line, repairing any breaks in the wire they came across. A small tree had fallen and taken out a large portion of the fence and they spent a half hour repairing it. Chase had brought along some leather gloves, which worked out well since she'd only brought hers and she'd really needed his help fixing the gap. If he hadn't joined her, she would have no doubt had to call for backup to repair the stretch.

Around lunchtime, they stopped and ate sandwiches under a large magnolia tree. Chase listened to her talk about running the ranch, then he talked about his time away from Fairplay, when he'd been in school and had worked at a vet clinic in upstate New York.

She'd been dying to ask if he'd been seeing anyone, but knew it was none of her business. Even though they'd technically been married for a little over seven years now, she still didn't think it was her right to ask. He continued talking and asked her questions about the ranch. He seemed very interested in the process of selling off her cattle in the fall.

"If you want, you can come with me when we drive them into Tyler to sell at auction next month."

"Really?" His eyebrows shot up. "I've never been to a cattle auction before. Once, in Boston, I went with a friend to an antique auction. It was so much fun that I ended up buying a wood statue of a dog holding a duck in its mouth for my dad." He laughed.

It ate at her all day, wondering if he'd gone to the auction with a girlfriend. It was on the tip of her tongue to ask him, but she bit her lip and kept reminding herself that just because she'd honored their vows, that didn't mean that he had done the same.

An hour before the sun set, they'd picked a spot along the fence line by a small stream which ran through the hills to pitch their tents and make camp. After raising her small tent, Lauren gathered a handful of wood for a campfire, then walked over to the stream, took off her boots, and put her feet in the water to cool off. Dingo splashed around happily on the muddy shore across the way.

Lauren was too preoccupied with her thoughts to hear Chase sneak up on her, but before she knew it, he'd pulled her into the waist-high water and had pulled her under, clothes and all.

Her breath was knocked out of her and when she came out of the water, she was sputtering and pulling her wet hair out of her eyes.

"What are you doing?" She tried not to squeal. Dingo wanted to join in the fun and chased around her, barking happily.

"We stink," he smiled, "so, I thought we'd clean up a little."

"Now my clothes are soaking wet." She stood in the middle of the water, her jeans hugging every curve. She looked down at herself and realized her white blouse and tank top were completely see-through and tried to pull them away from her body a little.

"They stink, too." He smiled and took off his own t-shirt and began washing it with a bar of soap he had in his hands. She held her breath at the view of his tan muscles as he worked to clean his clothes. When he was done, he held the soap out to her. "We can hang them on a branch and they'll be dry by morning."

She looked at the soap and realized she did probably stink, and besides, the cool water felt nice. "Fine." She sat down in the water, hoping it would cover most of her, then took off her top shirt and grabbed the soap from him. After scrubbing her shirt clean, she rung it out and tossed it onto the grass to hang up later. When she looked up,

Chase was standing along the shore facing away from her as he wrung out his jeans. Her breath was knocked out of her lungs for the second time in five minutes.

How did he get the muscles on his back and shoulders to be so toned? Her mind wandered for a moment, imagining running her fingers over each ridge. He was tan and his hair looked darker now that it was dripping wet. When he turned around, it took her a second to rip her eyes from his chest.

She saw him quickly smile before he started walking slowly towards her.

"Come on. You're turn."

"What?" She backed up a little.

"Those jeans smell of horse and dirt. It's time they came off and I got a look at what you have underneath." She held up her hands as she backed off.

"I can take my own pants off, thank you." He laughed at her.

"Trust me, you're going to need help. My jeans were loose and I had trouble. And since I've been looking at that fine ass of yours all day, I know your jeans are a lot tighter than mine were. Since water shrinks denim, we'll be lucky if we can get them off working together."

She held up her hands and he stopped walking. "Fine, try it then." He motioned for her to go ahead.

She did. As she sat in the waist high water, she tried with all her might to get the slippery denim to slide down her hips. Chase stood a few feet away from her and laughed. Then he walked over and put his hands under her arms and hauled her up.

"You can't possibly do this while sitting down." He looked down at her tank top and she realized he could see everything. His eyes heated and for a moment she totally forgot where they were and what it was they were trying to do. Then he blinked and focused on helping her slide the wet jeans off her hips and legs. It took them almost ten minutes and a lot of laughter, but they finally freed her legs from the tight material.

She was thankful that she was wearing a dark pair of cotton panties, so at least she had something to hide from his view.

They laughed and talked while floating in the small stream. Just before the sun finally sank below the trees, she walked to the edge of the stream and gathered her clothes.

"Leaving so soon?" He looked at her without getting up.

"I'll just start dinner." She tried not to look back. It had been hard enough being so close to him like this. She hadn't really relaxed and enjoyed the water. She was sure that the water was actually steaming off her body, and she knew her face was heated and probably red from what she was thinking.

Shaking their clothes out, she hung them neatly on a low branch. He'd been right. They were already almost completely dry and smelled a good deal better than before. She knew she did as well.

She gathered her boots and carefully walked back to her tent and pulled on her backup pair of jeans, then slid on a t-shirt over her almost dry tank top. Her hair was tangled a little and after starting a fire and putting a can of soup in the pan for dinner, she sat on a log. Dingo lay on the ground beside her as Lauren started combing her hair.

Minutes later, she watched Chase walk towards his bag with nothing but his boots and a wet pair of boxers on. He stood in one spot and balanced as he pulled each foot out of his boots and pulled up his pair of jeans. Then he put on another button up shirt, and started putting up his tent.

"You know, you could probably sleep three in there." She put another large stick on the fire and stirred the can of tomato soup she was heating up.

He looked over at her and smiled over his shoulder. "You're welcome to join me."

She was very thankful that it was probably too dark for him to see her face, because sitting there watching as he finished putting in the stakes for the tent, her mind kept playing a scene of them tangled in a large sleeping bag.

"That smells good." He finished his tent, then

walked over and sat on another log across from the fire and looked at her.

"Isn't it funny that when you're exposed to the elements, everything smells and tastes better?" She poured him a healthy bowl of soup, then helped herself to some. "I mean, having a can of tomato soup at home, cooked on a stove, it just doesn't taste this good." She took a spoonful and closed her eyes at the rich taste.

"I know what you mean. It could be that we worked our tails off today."

"Hmmm." She shook her head. "I think it's because man was made to be outside."

"Hunting and gathering?" He took a spoonful of his soup and smiled.

"Exactly." She pointed her spoon in his direction. "I mean, food is good inside, but out here"—she motioned around them—"you have the smells and sounds of nature around you."

"Our animal instincts kick in." His eyes heated.

She nodded and took a bite of the loaf of bread she'd brought along, tearing it with her teeth like an animal would, then smiling over at him. "Exactly," she said and he laughed.

By the time she settled down in her sleeping bag with Dingo to keep her company, she was exhausted. Every muscle in her body ached. The cool water had done little to relieve the tension that she had felt being so close to Chase all day.

She loved riding horses, but after six hours, anyone would have felt the effects. Not to mention all the work it had taken moving the fallen trees and fixing the barbed wire. When her head hit her pillow, she was out. In her dreams, she played over the image of Chase almost naked and dripping wet.

It was dark when she opened her eyes. She lay there for a few seconds trying to figure out what had woken her. Dingo vibrated next to her. The dog's low growls barely made any noise. Then she felt shivers run down her body as she realized there were no sounds outside her tent. The crickets that had been a steady rhythm in her ears all night, the croaking frogs, the owl that had occasionally hooted were now all silent. Everything was quiet. Too quiet. Grabbing her pistol, she held onto Dingo's collar and slowly crawled towards the zipper of her tent. Before she could reach it, it started to unzip. She pulled up her pistol and pointed it towards the opening. Flipping off the safety, she took a deep breath.

Chase lay in his large tent, listening to the night sounds. He just couldn't get Lauren out of his mind. He lay there thinking of a million excuses to crawl into her small tent. To feel his body next to her soft skin. To run his hands, his mouth, over every inch of her wonderful body. It had been pure torture bathing with her in the water, and he'd walked away with images that would forever be embedded in his mind.

He lay there imagining a million different scenarios then realized that all sound outside had stopped. He crawled to the opening of his tent and peeked out just as he saw a dark figure lean towards Lauren's tent. He was out of the tent and across the clearing in ten seconds flat. Sticks and rocks bit into the soles of his feet as he approached the figure from behind. The man was crouched down, unzipping Lauren's tent when Chase flew at him from the side.

"What the...?" He heard right before he landed with a grunt on his back. A large rock protruding from the ground struck him in the ribs and stole his breath for a moment. The man struggled to get out of Chase's hold and swung his elbow out, catching Chase in the jaw. Chase lost his hold for just a second, and in that second, the man gained his feet and started backing away quickly. Chase reached out and grabbed his pant legs.

"Stop!" he heard Lauren screaming. But he didn't stop since he could very well be fighting for his life and, more important, hers. "Chase, stop!"

Finally, her voice broke through the haze that had fogged his brain. When he released the man, he sprinted off into the trees at record speed. Chase watched as the darkness consumed the figure. He hadn't even gotten a good look at the man's face. Damn!

"You've scared him off." She stood over Chase, her pistol pointing in the direction the dark figure had just disappeared to. Her other hand was holding onto a very pissed and barking Dingo.

"What the hell?" He sat in the dirt, wiping at his nose. Blood was flowing from the corner of his mouth. "Grab a light, will you?" he asked, sitting in the dirt. She told the dog to stay then rummaged around in her tent for the small lantern she had. Dingo walked over to Chase and laid her head in his lap while he pet her between her ears.

When the light hit him, he heard her gasp. "Oh! You're bleeding." She rushed over to him and set the light on the rock that had jabbed him in the ribs a few seconds ago. Taking her outer shirt off, she used the edge of it to wipe at his mouth. He watched her sit close to him in nothing but a white tank top, the light of the lantern causing her skin to glow, and his mouth went completely dry.

She leaned over him, her face a breath away from him. Her hands shook as she wet the cloth and used it to clean his mouth.

"I'm okay, Lauren," he told her, not really wanting her to back away. She just kept talking about how stupid he was to jump the guy and that she'd had everything under control. He looked down at the loaded gun and the sleeping dog.

"What if it had been me?"

"What?" She stopped what she was doing and tilted her head and looked at him.

"What if it had been me trying to sneak into your tent?"

"It wasn't." She raised her hand to continue cleaning his lip, which at this point was completely clean.

"But it could have been."

She looked at him. "I wouldn't have shot you. I doubt I would have shot whoever that was either." She shrugged her shoulders.

He seriously doubted that. He'd seen her practice shooting in the makeshift shooting range her father had built on the side of the barn. She'd been raised around cattle and he knew for a fact that she'd had to put down several herself. But he let it slide this time.

"Who do you think that was?" She sat back and crossed her arms over her chest, then started rubbing them with her hands.

"Beats me." Even though the night air was still sticky with heat, he saw small goose bumps rise on her skin. Leaning over, he took a log and tossed it on the embers in their fire pit. Then he put a few smaller sticks and some leaves on it and got the fire going again. "Come over here." He patted the ground next to him. When she scooted over to him, he put his arm around her and leaned back onto the log.

"Do you think it was the same person who was hunting yesterday?"

"I doubt it. Maybe it was just someone who was lost, and thought they'd steal something." He doubted it, but she seemed to relax next to him.

"Thanks for coming to my rescue." She rested her head on his shoulder as he chuckled.

"Lady, you were packing heat. If anything, you came to mine." He felt her chuckle and pulled her closer.

"I don't think I can sleep anymore tonight," she mumbled.

"If you want, you're welcome to join me in my tent." When she pulled back and looked at him, he smiled. "I'll be good. Scout's honor." He held up his hand and made the Scout's secret oath.

"That would be nice. But I want to sit here for a while longer. For some reason, I'm chilled."

"Shock," he said and pulled her closer. "I'm a little cold myself, even though it's probably still in the high seventies tonight."

She sighed and rested her head back against his chest. He started running a hand over her hair, enjoying the feel of it.

"Talk to me. Get my mind off what just happened."

"Hmm, okay. I've decided to keep Buddy, the three-legged dog. My dad tells me it's about time I had a dog of my own. He says it shows everyone in town that I'm back to stay and that I'm ready to settle down." He chuckled at that. "Funny, that's the main reason I came back to town, anyway."

"Are you really? I mean, I've heard people talking at the diner and they all say the same thing about you and Grant. Everyone thinks that you'll both be gone within the year."

He smiled. He'd heard the rumors going around as well. He thought that it was the main reason for her hesitance in building a relationship with him. "Yeah, funny. I talked to Grant the other morning over breakfast, and we both agreed that wild horses couldn't drag either of us out of town again. Don't get me wrong, city life was nice for a while. But after sitting in traffic every morning, standing in line for thirty minutes to get a cup of coffee, or just having to deal with finding a parking spot at the grocery store, you kind of get tired of it all." He looked off into the fire and stroked her hair as he spoke. "I like walking into Mama's and having a hot cup in my hands in less than a minute. Or parking in the front spot at the Grocery Stop." He chuckled. "And the last time Fairplay saw a traffic jam was when that herd of cattle ran down Main Street fifteen years ago." She laughed at that. "No, I like it right where I am." He wrapped his arms around her.

"Me, too." She sighed and settled more deeply

Jill Sanders

into his arms.

Chapter Nine

Lauren woke to the feeling of Chase kissing her neck. She snuggled into him and wrapped her arms around his naked shoulders as his mouth moved slowly over every inch of her shoulders. His hands were on her hips and when he started moving them higher, she held her breath. He pulled her shirt up a little, exposing her stomach to the cool morning air. His fingers played over the line of her jeans, tugging until they rode low on her hips so he could run a finger lightly over her exposed skin.

"Tell me to stop," he mumbled against her skin.

She shook her head. "No, don't." She buried her fingers into his hair and pulled his mouth to hers. The kiss was heated and she felt her toes curl as he took it deeper, pulling her under as his hands tugged on her jeans.

He slid them slowly down her hips and off her legs. Her cotton panties were still in place and he pulled back and looked down at her. Her tank top was hiked up, showing most of her stomach. She was sure her hair was in a ball of knots.

"So beautiful." His eyes roamed over every inch of her. Her breath hitched as he ran a finger lightly over her ribs. He looked into her eyes as his fingers traveled lower, pulling at the rim of her panties. She moaned and closed her eyes, tilting her head back as he slowly exposed more of her skin.

She'd never been this exposed before. The morning sun was streaming into the netted roof of his tent. The bright colors flooded her senses as he gently pulled aside the cotton and touched her with his fingertips. Her shoulders bounded off the sleeping bag and she let a low moan escape her lips as more colors exploded behind her closed eyelids. He placed a hand on her stomach to hold her still.

"My god," she thought he'd said, but she was too busy to ask as she felt him touch her where no one had before.

She was a live wire. He couldn't get enough of

her. The bright colors of the sunrise were streaming into the small tent and he wished more than anything to freeze this moment in his brain forever. Her dark hair was pooled over the sleeping bag, and her lips were pink and swollen from his kisses as she lightly bit on her bottom lip to keep herself from screaming. Her skin glowed in the daylight and he wished they had hours so he could explore every inch, taste every inch. When he pulled down her cotton panties and exposed her pink skin, then ran a finger gently over her, he was surprised when she exploded and melted in his hands. She was even more beautiful during orgasm than he'd ever imagined. If he did this to her with just a simple touch, what would she do when he finally made love to her?

It took all his willpower to pull her clothes back on her as she recovered. He knew there was a time and place for everything and getting Lauren in bed was something he wanted to save for the right time, the right place.

"Chase? Aren't you..."

"Shhh, there's plenty of time later." He pulled her close and kissed her eyes and face. "You're so beautiful. Your hair sparkles in the morning light."

She chuckled.

"What?" He leaned up and looked down into her face. "Did I say something funny?"

Her eyes slid open slowly and she smiled up at

him. "It's all very funny. You. Me. Here. Like this."

"What's so funny about it?" He leaned down and placed a soft kiss on her nose.

"Well, there for a moment it actually sounded like you were going to start spouting poetry."

He smiled. "So, maybe I feel like giving you poetry." He leaned back further as she pulled herself up onto her elbows.

"Johnathan Chase Graham, the second." He winched at his full name. "I doubt you would know a line of poetry if it sprouted teeth and bit you on your arse." She smiled at him.

"I think that I shall never see," he began with a smile, "a poem as lovely as a tree."

She laughed and listened patiently to the whole poem, then clapped her hands when he was done. He loved her eyes when she smiled. They completed his day and he couldn't help but smile back at her.

"Very well, I stand corrected." She sat across from him, her knees tucked under her as she pulled on her t-shirt.

By lunchtime, he was wishing for another dip in the stream. Not only was it hotter than yesterday, but they had found and repaired three large holes in the fence. They'd had to haul a dozen or so large branches off the wires and she'd even produced an ax so he could chop some of the larger pieces up so they could move them away from the fence line.

They sat in the shade of a cluster of trees and he gulped down as much water as he could to cool his body. Finally, he took a handful and splashed himself over the head and face. Even Dingo had given up and lay in the shade, choosing not to run around chasing squirrels.

"I can't believe you thought you could do this all by yourself." He looked over at her. Sweat streamed down her face, causing her hair to stick to the sides of her neck and face.

"Well, usually there aren't this many downed trees." She looked up and down the fence line and frowned. "We had beetles come through here last year and a lot of the pines were killed off." She pointed to a dozen or more dead pines that stood in the distance. "I suppose I'll have to pay someone to come back and clear out some of the larger ones. Otherwise we'll be doing this all over again in a few months."

He smiled. He didn't know if she realized it, but she'd included him in her future plans.

After lunch, they headed across the field and started making their way back to the house. By the time they made it down the hills, the sun was already set and they had to let the horses lead them across the field to the barn. When he dismounted from Buster, he realized that his ass wasn't the only thing asleep on him. His legs felt like jelly and he was sure there were blisters on the insides of his thighs from the saddle.

He'd been raised riding horses, but had never ridden this much in a two-day stretch before. He walked over and helped Lauren down from her horse, knowing that if he felt this bad, she probably did as well. She wrapped her arms around his neck and smiled up at him.

"I always love coming home after a long peaceful trip." She reached up on her toes and kissed him. He lost himself in the moment, his aches and pains totally forgotten as her mouth traveled over his. He leaned closer to her and bumped her back into the horse as he deepened the kiss. The horse snorted and pushed them back until he had to catch himself and her to keep them from falling. They laughed, then got to work putting the horses away for the night. It took almost two hours for him to get back to his place. When he walked in, he fell onto the couch and was unconscious in under a minute.

The next morning he woke to pounding on his door. He yanked the door open, preparing to yell at whoever was on the other side, but caught himself when he saw Haley standing on the porch, a squirming Buddy in her hands.

"Good morning. We figured you would be up by now." She handed him Buddy and looked over his shoulder into the small house.

"Thanks for watching him," he said in between dog kisses.

"Oh, he was no problem at all. I even taught him a few tricks while you were gone." She smiled and he realized how much she looked like Lauren. They had the same hair, eyes, and smile. He couldn't help but smile back at her.

"Yeah? What kind of tricks?" He set the little dog down as Haley walked past him, into the living room.

"I've never been in one of the ranch hand places before." She stood in the middle of the floor and did a quick circle. "Nice." Then she called for Buddy and he quickly rushed to her side. "Sit," she said in a soft voice, and to his surprise, the small dog sat on its bottom, its tail wagging a million miles per hour. "Lay." The dog quickly lay down and looked up at her. "Good boy, now stay." She pointed to the ground, then turned and walked down the small hallway to his bedroom door. Buddy watched her, his tail still thumping the ground. When she disappeared, he let out a low whine. Then, from the other room, she called, "Come." Buddy bounded up and ran as fast as his three legs would carry him into the next room.

Haley walked in, holding Buddy in her arms, smiling.

"We still need to work on a few others, but he's a smart one. Aren't you?" The small dog licked her on the face as she laughed.

"I can't thank you enough for watching him."

"Oh, it was no trouble at all." She handed him back the dog. "Besides, Lauren told us what happened the other night."

For a moment his mind went blank and all he could think about was Lauren lying naked in his sleeping bag.

Then she continued. "About someone trying to break into her tent."

"Oh," he recovered. "Yeah. Well, she handled that pretty well all by herself."

"Yes, well. Alex and I don't like it when she disappears up to the hills all alone like that. We've been telling her for years that there are vagrants living up there. Do you know that I overheard your father telling Mr. Holton that there were actual moonshiners up in those hills? Then, just a few years back, I guess, the sheriff caught a group of men growing marijuana plants." She shook her head and crossed her arms over her chest. He noticed that Haley was a little taller than Lauren and about twenty pounds skinnier. He smiled a little and realized he liked Lauren's extra curves.

"Well, it's a good thing you went along, anyway. She was pretty upset about the state of the fence and just this morning she hired the Johnston brothers to clear the line of all the pine's the beetles killed last season." She started walking towards his door. "Thanks again for watching out for my sister."

"Anytime." He smiled. "Thanks for looking out for Buddy."

"Anytime." She smiled and closed his door behind her.

He turned and looked down at the small dog. "Buddy, is it possible to fall in love with someone's family, too?" The small dog tilted his head, like he was trying to understand what Chase was saying. Then he realized that he'd said it out loud. He'd known for years how he felt about Lauren. Hell, when he'd proposed marriage seven years ago, he'd known that he loved her. But it was a different kind of love than what he was feeling now. Now he wanted her completely and he knew he needed to set out to show her how much she needed him. He knew he needed a plan, and he decided there was no time like the present.

Walking to the back, he decided a shower and a shave were first on his list.

She was running late. She hated to be late. At least when it came to her time off. It wasn't very often that she took a night off to enjoy herself.

"Can't this thing go any faster?" Alex sat next to her, checking the mirror on the back of the truck's visor. Lauren knew that her sister's makeup was perfect. After all, she'd spent the last two hours getting ready. Lauren had spent a quarter of that time and thought she looked just as nice. She quickly checked herself in the rear view mirror and smiled at her reflection.

"Sit back. We'll get there in time for you to get up on stage." Thursday night at The Rusty Rail was karaoke night, and Alex loved to get up on stage and sing. And for the most part, everyone in town loved to hear her sing. Alex was the only one of the sisters that had gained their mother's sweet voice.

Lauren could remember her mother singing in the kitchen as she baked or while trying to put Haley down for a nap. Alex's soothing voice reminded her so much of her mother, sometimes it hurt to hear her singing in the house.

She glanced over at her sisters. Haley sat in the middle, quietly gazing ahead. She wore a pretty green dress and boots. Lauren knew that her sister liked to dance as much as she did and she started really looking forward to having some fun for once.

Alex's coat covered whatever she was wearing underneath. Lauren knew it was probably something she wouldn't approve of, but years ago, she'd stopped trying to fight her sister on her wardrobe choices. Alex was going to wear whatever she wanted, and all Lauren could do was try to keep her from going too far.

The short jean skirt she wore was probably the most modest thing she was wearing that night. She was also wearing her bright white cowgirl boots. Lauren thought about her own long white skirt and simple blue top. She was never one to dress fancy, but she did like dressing up a little every now and then. Her brown boots were her finest and she only wore them for special occasions, like tonight.

She knew Chase was going to be at the Rusty Rail and wanted more than anything to dance with him again.

Finally, they pulled into the packed parking lot of the old barn building. The Rusty Rail sat right next to the old railroad tracks. In its earlier days, it had been a stock room for unloading animals off the railways. In the early sixties, BJ, the current owner's father, had purchased the old place and had turned it into a country bar. Once her daddy had passed on, BJ had turned it into what it was today—a town gathering place where music played and families gathered, where you could grab a cold beer.

When they pulled up, Travis Nolan, Alex's long-standing boyfriend was standing out front, smoking. When he saw them drive up, he flipped his cigarette across the sidewalk and slowly started walking towards them. Alex met him halfway and jumped into his arms and gave him a long kiss.

"Looks like they're back on again. I don't like

him," Haley said, sitting beside her still.

"Me either, but if we say anything, it'll only make her want him more." Lauren and Haley sighed and got out of the truck together.

Inside the music was loud and the place was crowded. The first Thursday of every month was always like this, especially in the summer and fall months. People wanted to wind down after a long, hot day's work.

"I'll see you later." Haley waved towards some of her friends and quickly disappeared, leaving Lauren standing at the door all by herself.

"Well, hello there, beautiful." His voice sent heat down her entire body. How could a man have so much power over her?

She turned and smiled up at him. He wore dark crisp jeans and a pressed white shirt that showed just how tan he was. When he smiled, his teeth shined in the dim light. Not even his belt buckle seemed that shiny. He pulled back his black Stetson in a gesture of respect and grabbed her arm lightly. The dimple near his mouth looked very inviting.

"I was hoping I'd run into you." She smiled up at him as they walked towards the dance floor. Already the small floor was packed. Everyone was dancing to the loud music that pumped out of the big speakers. When they got to the dance floor, Chase pulled her close and started smoothly moving across the old wood floor. It was a simple dance that they'd danced plenty of times before. She loved dancing, but she especially loved it with Chase.

While his hand rested on her lower back, the other holding hers gently, she remembered the first time he'd pulled her onto the dance floor. It had been in sixth grade. She'd been taller than him, then, which was a fact that she remembered so well because she'd had to look down into his eyes as they learned the movements in gym class. She also remembered holding his sweaty hand and wanting nothing more than to let go and wipe the moisture off on her jeans. Now she looked up into his smiling eyes and marveled at the warmth of his dry hand and how his touch made her feel. So much had changed since that first dance. They had both changed. She smiled up at him and let herself be carried across the floor smoothly.

Less than an hour later, she made her way to the crowded woman's restroom and was surprised to see Alex there, crowded by several of her friends. She had a large smile on her face and she was showing off a ring.

"What?" Lauren pushed her way through the crowd. "What's this?" She grabbed her sister's hand and barely noticed as everyone quickly left the small room.

"Travis proposed. Isn't it wonderful?" Her sister beamed down at the small ring.

"No." She shook her head and grabbed her sister's hand and looked into her eyes. "No, it's not."

Alex yanked her hand away and frowned at her. "Why can't you just be happy for me?"

"Because you don't belong with someone like Travis. Everyone in town knows he's no good. That you're not good together." She wanted to take her sister's shoulders and shake her to make her understand that she was making a huge mistake.

"I don't care what you think. You're just jealous." Her sister crossed her arms over her chest and glared at her just as Haley walked into the small bathroom.

"I heard..." she started to say, but dropped off when she saw what was going on.

"Tell her, Haley. Tell her what a mistake she's making." Lauren motioned towards Alex.

"Lauren, it's not really my place." Haley started to back out the open door.

"Oh no, you don't." Lauren turned on Haley. "I've listened to your opinions of Travis for years now. It's high time you told your big sister what your thoughts are on Travis Nolan. Why don't you tell Alexis about the time Travis cornered you in the barn? Or the time..."

"Shut up!" Alex yelled, and Lauren spun around and glared at her. "I can't believe you are going to stand here and ruin the happiest night in my life."

Alex walked over and stuck her face in front of Lauren's. Lauren could see her sister was mad. Alex had such pale skin that when she was upset, she turned a dark red, which caused her brown eyes to look like they had a hint of red in them. "I'm going to walk out of this room and this will be the last time I expect to hear a negative word about me marrying Travis. Is that clear?" Alex looked between Lauren and Haley. Haley quickly nodded and Alex turned back to her.

"I can't make that promise," she said and crossed her arms over her chest. "I'm responsible for you and I don't approve. I'll do what it takes to prove to you that this is all a big mistake."

"You are not responsible for me or for Haley. I don't know why you think you have to take everything on all by yourself—the ranch, the house, us. You don't. We don't want you butting into our lives. We're actually quite sick of you running everything. Just step back and get off our backs for once." Alex stormed out of the bathroom, leaving Lauren gazing at the spot where her sister had just been. She didn't realize she was crying until Haley walked over and pulled her into a hug.

"I'm sorry she said that."

"Is it true?" She pulled back a little and looked at her youngest sister. Haley was taller than her and she had to look up slightly.

"No." Her sister shook her head. "Lauren,

you've done so much since mom died. Then after dad..." She shook her head more and closed her eyes. "I know Alex and I haven't been very much help, but we try. We love the ranch as much as you do. I think if you'd just give us a chance, you'd see that we can help out more. We want to help out more. Alex will see through Travis sooner or later. Don't worry."

"I just hope it's sooner rather than later. I can't let her marry him." She turned and looked at the door, trying to figure out how to prove to her sister that the town's bad boy was not husband material for anyone.

When Haley and Lauren walked out of the restroom, they both stopped and listened. Alex was on stage singing Patsy Cline's, "Always," while Travis stood close by, smiling. The crowd was eating it up, with the exception of Haley and Lauren.

Before the song was over, Lauren turned and marched out of the crowded building, slamming the door behind her. The cool night air hit her and she wrapped her arms around herself. There was less than a month to go before the leaves would be changing colors and falling. Looking off to the dark southern sky, she could tell they were in for a storm soon.

She walked a few yards over to the old log fence that separated the walkway and the train tracks. Leaning against it, she closed her eyes and took a deep breath. She had been standing out there for a few minutes before she realized the sound had changed. She looked around and didn't see anyone, but the feeling outside was different. Like she was being watched. She turned to go and saw Chase walk out the front door. He stopped and looked around and when he saw her, he started walking towards her.

"Hey?" he said as soon as he got close enough. "Are you okay?"

She blinked a few tears away, then nodded.

"I heard about Alex and Travis," he said.

"And?" she sighed.

He shrugged his shoulders and put his hands deep into his jean pockets. She turned back around, disgusted. Travis Nolan was no good. Just because his daddy was the town's mayor and had been for as long as she could remember didn't mean he was anything like his father. Actually, Travis was the farthest thing from it. He'd been arrested twice on drinking and driving in the past two years. Both times, he'd walked away the next morning after his father had marched in and bailed him out. She was sure he'd been arrested a few more times, but didn't know all the particulars. But what had really set her opinion of Travis was when she'd walked in on him once when he'd cornered Haley in their barn. He'd had his hand on her sister's breast, squeezing it. She'd grabbed up a pitchfork and had threatened him with castration if she ever found him on her land again. Since then, he'd made excuses to Alex about why he couldn't come out to the house.

"He's no good for her," Lauren said under her breath.

"I know it and you know it. Hell, the whole town knows it, but that's not going to stop them from making their own choices." He put a hand on her shoulder, gently rubbing the tension in her muscles.

She enjoyed it for just a second before she turned on him. "I'm in charge of them. There ought to be something I can do to stop this."

He shook his head and bent down and placed his forehead on hers. "They need to cut their own path. Hopefully, they'll wake up before it's too late. I mean, it's not like they're going to go down to the courthouse and get hitched tomorrow."

She winced, knowing that's exactly what they had done seven years ago.

"Travis' mother will want the biggest wedding the county has ever seen, which will take a while to plan." He pulled her back into his arms. It felt too good to pull out of his warmth, so she stood there with his arms wrapped around her, looking off at the star-filled sky, listening to the music stream out of the building behind them.

Chapter Ten

Chase felt Lauren relax against his chest and wished the night would go on forever. She felt so good next to him, and she smelled sweet as he placed soft kisses along her hairline. It was all he could do not to pull her into a dark corner and take what he wanted from her. She sighed and slowly turned towards him, wrapping her arms around his shoulders. Then she slipped up onto her toes and started placing soft kisses along his jaw line. His eyes slid closed as he pulled her lips up to his.

He backed her up a step until she was pinned between him and the fence. His hands roamed over her until he couldn't stand anymore. The light material of her skirt and top did little to hide her curves. He wished they weren't just a few steps from the largest crowd in Fairplay.

"Lauren." He pulled back and cupped her face

so she would look up at him. "Come back to my place with me tonight." He held his breath, waiting for her response. Her eyes fluttered open and for just a moment, he thought she would say yes. Then she closed her eyes and shook her head.

"I can't." She let out a deep sigh and rested her head on his shoulder. "I wish it was all that easy, but I just can't right now."

He pulled back a little more as she snuggled into his chest. Looking off towards the town, he wished he had someone to blame, but knew the mess she was in was more his fault than anyone else's.

"How about we go back in and get a few more dances in?" He closed his mind to the possibilities of the night and settled his mind on just enjoying every moment he could with her.

She looked up at him and smiled. "I'd like that."

Two hours later, Chase drove up to the little house alone. It had been years since he'd been with anyone. To be honest, it felt longer when he was with Lauren. He couldn't seem to control his desires and felt like he was fumbling around like a high school kid instead of a man almost in his thirties. When he got out of the truck, he heard a loud noise off toward the next little house in the row of ranch houses.

Loud voices carried across the empty space and he listened for a while as two men argued. When he heard fists hitting bone, he rushed towards the noises to break up the fight. He didn't expect to see Jimmy, Lauren's foreman, lying in the porch light on the ground with a younger, but much larger, man sitting on top of him, pummeling him til the older man was no doubt unconscious.

"Hey." He rushed over to the side of the house and started pulling the larger man off Lauren's foreman. "Knock it off." It took some doing, but finally he pulled the man off. When the heavyset man started swinging in his direction, Chase planted two quick jabs into his ribs and sent the man falling back two steps.

Jimmy moaned and Chase looked down at the man for a split second. He didn't see the blow that took him down, but woke a few minutes later to Jimmy shaking him. "You okay, Chase?" Chase shook his head clear and tried to focus his eyes.

"Son of a..."

"Hey now, it's not his mother's fault." Jimmy sat in the dirt next to him. "That boy is the spawn of his father. My sister tried the best she could. Nothing would have turned that boy around." Jimmy shook his head and leaned his hands on his knees.

"I'm sorry, Jimmy."

The foremen looked over at him. "Don't worry about it." He started to get up and Chase rushed to help him stand. He'd been cold cocked, but the other man had been pummeled. "Well, come on in and get cleaned up. I might have a beer in the fridge for you."

"Thanks." Chase followed Jimmy past the other buildings until they reached the first and largest of the houses. He knew that Jimmy had been foremen on the ranch since Lauren's father had run the place. Other than that, he didn't know much about the man.

He followed Jimmy through the door and noticed how clean the place was. It looked like a woman lived there. There were small yellow pillows on the bright blue couches, a vase of flowers sitting on the coffee table, and there was even a small, white lace doily sitting underneath the vase. He didn't think that Jimmy was married. Maybe he was seeing someone?

"BJ likes to stop by a few days during the week," Jimmy said when he noticed Chase's attention to the feminine details. "We've been seeing each other for a few years now." He smiled and tested his jaw a few times. "Damn kid almost took my jaw off." His smile fell away.

"What were you two fighting about?" Chase took the cold beer Jimmy handed him and popped the top and took a drink. The cold fluid felt wonderful on his back teeth, which still felt rattled.

"This and that." Jimmy shrugged his shoulders. "I found out he was stealing from the other hands and fired him. I guess he was pissed."

Jimmy walked over and grabbed a cloth off the counter, then sat down on the couch. Setting his beer down on the coffee table, he started wiping the blood off his mouth, then put a bag of frozen peas on his face.

"There's no cause to beat someone up. Here..." Chase set his beer down and walked over to the other man. "I better have a look. You could have a concussion."

"Naw, I've been on the losing end of plenty of fights. Had plenty of concussions falling off a bronco before, as well. I'm just rattled a bit. I guess it hurts more when it's family doing the swinging." He shook his head and Chase sat next to him on the couch.

"Yeah, I remember getting into a fight with my cousins once. They live east of here a ways. I don't get to see them often, but a dozen years back one of them started talking bad about someone I knew and the next thing I knew I was on top of him. He was twice my size at the time and a few years older, so naturally I didn't stay on top for long." Chase smiled a little. "But a few days later, we made up and everything fell back into place."

Jimmy shook his head. "I don't think Hewitt is one to easily forget. Besides, I knew when I hired him on that the boy was pure trouble. I should have sent him packing when he disappeared last weekend."

Chase's mind cleared a little. "Last weekend?

The weekend Lauren went up to the cabin?"

"Yeah, I'd taken all the hands to the east ridge. We'd lost a lot of the pine trees along there to beetles last year." He shook his head. "It was a mess. Had to practically rebuild the whole damned fence. Anyway, Saturday morning I went to check up on Hewitt and he was gone. Stayed gone until we got back to the ranch and found him sitting in the loft, drunk as a skunk."

Chase thought back to the man who'd tried to break into Lauren's tent. It could have been Hewitt, but it had been too dark to really know.

As he walked back to his place, Chase couldn't stop comparing the man from last weekend with Hewitt. Had they been the same man? Jimmy mentioned that he'd fired Hewitt, which was a good thing. He would just have to make sure the man was gone first thing tomorrow. He didn't like knowing that it could have been a lot worse had he not gone along with Lauren. He walked around his small rooms for a while. Buddy was curled up on the dog bed Chase had bought for him. The bowl of food and water sat next to it. The small dog had put on a few pounds since he'd rescued him. He knew he'd have to watch his weight since he only had three legs, but he could still use a few more pounds to get to a healthy size.

Chase switched on the TV set, but his mind just wouldn't shut down, so he decided a nice long walk would do him some good. Grabbing his light jacket, he headed out, not knowing he was aiming for the main house.

Lauren sat on the front porch swing, waiting for Alex to get home. She didn't like the way she'd handled things and wanted to talk to her sister and try to smooth everything out. She'd showered and changed out of her skirt and blouse and had put on her comfortable cotton Dallas Cowboys PJ bottoms and a t-shirt. She had grabbed her dad's cotton pullover as she walked out the front door to ward off the chill in the air.

She could see the clouds building in the night sky and knew that by tomorrow evening they'd have heavy rain. The fields could use the break and so could she. Late summer rains were the best. Even though the temperature hardly ever dropped lower than seventy even after a storm, it was still a nice change from the pounding heat that came every day.

Her mind sharpened when headlights turned into the driveway. She frowned a little when she saw it was Travis's truck. It stopped a few yards back from the house, and she could see her sister waving her hands around, then she got out of the passenger side of the truck and slammed the door.

The truck spun out in the gravel and took off back down the drive at high speeds.

"He hates it that you wait up for me, you know."

Lauren smiled a little as her sister stepped onto the porch. "I know."

Her sister leaned on the railing and crossed her arms, then tilted her head. "You're not my mother, you know."

"I've never claimed to be. I just want what's best for everyone."

"And you think Travis isn't what's best for me?" For the first time in months, she could see her sister thinking about things.

Lauren took a deep breath and released it. "I think you're still young enough to find someone who fits you perfectly. Like what mom and dad had."

"I can barely remember them together." Alex looked off towards the barn. Lauren stood up and walked over to her sister, putting her arms around her.

"They used to dance in the kitchen. She'd be humming a tune and he'd sweep her off her feet with a kiss."

Alex chuckled. "I remember walking in once and seeing her slap dad's hands out of her cookie batter." Lauren smiled.

"They never fought. Dad never raised his voice to her. Lauren turned her sister until she looked directly in her eyes. "And Dad never cheated on mom."

Alex pulled back a little. "Travis has never cheated on me. The one time he did get with someone else, we'd broken up. But now that we're back together..."

Lauren shook her head. "I'm not going to stand here and tell you what's right for you. I realize it's not my place. Just know that I love you, sister. You have to find the right man for you. The one that's going to make your knees weak and turn your insides to jelly." They smiled at each other.

"Mom always used to say that about dad." Lauren nodded in agreement.

"That's what she wanted for us. All of us."

Alex stood there for a moment, then hugged her and kissed her on the cheek.

"Thanks. Good night." Alex walked to the door and pulled the screen door open, then stopped and looked back at her. "Lauren?"

"Yes?"

"I see what Chase does to you. Don't be fooled. That man is crazy for you and I think...I *know* you feel the same way about him." She smiled and pulled the front door closed behind her.

Lauren leaned against the railing and wrapped

her arms around herself, thinking of Chase.

"Is she right?" came a deep voice behind her.

Lauren squealed, and spun around. All the air in her lungs got knocked out of her. Dingo let out a happy bark and rushed to his side. The dog was always letting him sneak up on her.

"What are you doing here?" she asked as he stepped into the light of the porch. Then she noticed the large bruise running down the left side of his jaw. "Oh!" She rushed over to him. "How did this happen?"

He let her turn his head so she could get a better view of the bruise. "Are you trying to avoid answering my question?" He smiled down at her.

"Don't be silly. Who did this to you?"

"It doesn't matter. Answer the question, Lauren." He pulled her closer, and she could feel his body vibrating. "Are you crazy about me?"

She pulled back a little. "It depends. I suppose there are some moments that you do make me a little crazy." She smiled.

"I'm crazy about you." He smiled a little and pulled her closer, running his hands in her hair. "I love the feel of your hair." He leaned closer. "The smell of you. The feel of you next to me." He brushed a kiss over her forehead, and she closed her eyes on a moan. "I couldn't shut down for the night, couldn't stop thinking about you." Then he trailed his mouth down to hers. Her mind shut off, her body turned on, and she was vibrating in his arms. He'd always done this to her, from that first kiss so many years ago on their wedding day.

He backed her up until her knees hit the railing, then he pulled her up so she sat on the wide rail. Her feet dangled on either side of his legs as he stepped in between them. On their own, her legs wrapped around his hips, pulling him closer to her as his hands roamed over her shoulders and hair.

"You taste so good," he moaned as he rained kisses down her neck. "I can't seem to get enough." She tilted her head back, exposing more skin for him to explore.

Her mind had spun so many fairy tales over the years, but nothing compared to how Chase made her feel when he whispered in her ear about much he enjoyed her. How much he wanted her.

"Come with me." He pulled back all of a sudden. He held out his hand and looked at her.

"Where?" She put her hands behind her back and he smiled even more.

"Don't you trust me?"

She shook her head and he laughed. "Fair enough." He picked up the rubber boots that sat by the door and set them in front of her. "I want to walk with you for a while."

"Walk?" She frowned a little. She was enjoying making out with him too much to think about going for a walk right now.

He leaned closer and whispered a little. "Lauren, your sisters are probably watching from those dark windows. Let's take a walk so we can have a little more privacy."

Her mind cleared. She realized that he was probably right. She looked at the large dark living room window and could just imagine her sisters sitting on the back of the couch, watching their every move.

Quickly putting on the boots, she took his offered hand and started walking into the dark night. The clouds had made their way over the moon, so the walking was slow going. When they had made it half way to the barn, Lauren turned him in the opposite direction.

"Trust me," she said and pulled him towards the backyard. When she stopped in front of the storm shelters doors, he chuckled and leaned down to open the large door.

Lauren easily made it to the bottom of the stairs and waited until she heard him shut the door before she reached over and flipped on the dim light.

He looked around the small room and smiled. It had been remodeled a few years back. Alex had gotten it in her mind that she was going to live here instead of in the main house. She'd spent a few days moving things around and pulling an old bed out here, and she had even filled it with scented candles.

Chase walked over and pulled a few candles off a shelf and lit them. Then he switched off the dim light as lavender scent and soft candlelight filled the small space.

"I like it." He smiled then walked back over to where she stood, nervously twisting her fingers in the hem of her shirt.

Jill Sanders

Chapter Eleven

Chase looked across the small space at Lauren and caught his breath. Her dark hair was flowing in light curls around her shoulders, and even in her Dallas Cowboys pajamas, she was something to look at. The light cotton clung to her every curve. He walked over and started to pull her jacket off. She moved to help him, but he pushed her hands aside.

"Let me." He used his fingertips to slowly unzip the zipper all the way, then took the hem of the jacket and pulled it up over her head.

She wore a white cotton t-shirt with Cowboys written over her breasts. The material was so light, he could see through it. Again, she'd stolen his breath away with her simplicity.

"You are so beautiful." He pulled her into his arms as she laughed.

"I should be wearing something silk and flowing." She frowned a little. "This is perfect. I'm a huge Dallas Cowboy's fan." He smiled as she chuckled.

"Well"—she bit her lip—"at least we have candlelight."

"I wouldn't want this any other way." He leaned down and took her mouth, slowly deepening the kiss until his knees felt weak. Then he started backing her up to the small bed that sat along the back wall. It was a single bed, only built for one, but they would just have to make do. When the back of her knees hit it, he pulled her down with him.

She chuckled a little when he had to adjust their position until finally there was enough room for him to pull her closer. Her back was against the wall, and her left leg hung over his hip. Just where he wanted her.

He kissed her until they were both out of breath, using his tongue to show her what he wanted to do to her soft body below. His hands slowly roamed over her shirt until she moaned and leaned back, giving him permission to explore the sensitive skin below.

Slowly he pulled her shirt up, exposing inch after inch of soft, milky skin. Stopping just below her perfect breasts, he dipped his head and tasted how perfect she was. He ran his tongue over every inch he'd just exposed as she twisted and moaned under him. When he reached the bottom of the shirt, he used his mouth to pull it up further, exposing the most perfect pair of breasts he'd ever seen. Leaning back, he looked down at her and lost his heart.

Her hair was fanned out over the white pillowcase. Her green eyes were clouded and her cheeks were flushed and pink, making her lips look a deeper shade of pink.

"Please." She put her hands into his hair and pulled him back to her. He ran his mouth over her puckered skin, dipping his tongue out to lap at her perfect nipples, finally taking one in to suckle on it. Her shoulders came off the bed as she cried out his name.

He lost a little control and quickly moved his hands lower, pulling down the loose band of her PJ's, until he found her underneath, wet and swollen for him. His fingers played over every inch as she called out for him over and over. Then his mouth trailed down, following the same path, until finally he ran his tongue over the sensitive skin, causing her to grip his hair tightly. He lapped her perfect lips until she cried out and he couldn't stand any more.

Then she was tugging his jacket off his shoulders. He quickly sat up and tossed it and his shirt to the floor. She smiled and pulled him back to her. He leaned in and smiled as he pulled her shirt up and over her head. Her smile faltered a little, but he leaned in and nuzzled her neck and he felt goose bumps raising all over her skin.

Her fingers were exploring his muscles, traveling lower on his stomach until she reached the snap of his jeans. She quickly ran her palm over his desire, over the course jean material, and had his eyes crossing. Pulling back a little, he took her hands in his and pulled them up and away.

"Chase, I want to..."

"Shhh, I know. I'm trying to go slow here." He smiled down at her. "If you keep doing that, I can't promise you I can."

"I don't care. I'm burning up. Please." She twisted a little under his hold. Then her tongue darted out and she slowly ran it over her bottom lip, her deep green eyes watching him as she teased him.

"Vixen." He smiled quickly, then took her mouth with his again. She tugged on his hands until he let her wrists go, then she was pulling his zipper down and yanking his jeans off his hips. It would have worked out great, but she hit a snag when his jeans hit his boots. He chuckled and sat up to take them off, tossing them across the room. Then he stood and yanked his pants down, making sure to set his wallet on the small table next to the bed. He'd need the condoms he always carried in it, later.

Her smile wavered when she saw him. He

actually saw her move away, closer to the wall. Looking down at her, he smiled.

"I won't hurt you." He knelt next to her on the bed and pulled her up to kneel in front of him. Her eyes stayed focus on his erection.

"Doesn't that hurt when it's so...large?" She blinked then looked up at him quickly.

He chuckled a little and shook his head. "I ache for you. I suppose it's painful wanting." He took her hand in his, then placed her hand on his shaft. She flinched a little, but when he moved his hand away, she smiled a little.

"Your skin is so soft. Yet you're so hard underneath." Her fingers glided over his skin, exploring.

He leaned his head back and groaned. "You're killing me." Her exploration stopped and he looked at her. She had a frown on her face and there was a crease between her brows. "In a good way," he finished. "Let me show you what you do to me."

Lauren's eyes closed as his fingers traced a line down her skin, swirling around each nipple until they puckered towards him. She swayed a little and his other hand moved to her shoulder to steady her. His fingers moved down over her stomach, dipping quickly into her belly button, then out again. When he pulled lightly on her bottoms and removed them, she sucked in a breath as his fingers dipped lower, running over her sensitive skin. She could feel the moisture between her legs and for a moment wondered if he knew she was hot for him.

"You're so hot and wet. Just waiting for me." He leaned in and kissed the side of her neck, sending ripples down her skin. With his fingertips, he played with her lips, using the moisture to dip his finger slowly in and out of her. She moaned and gripped his shoulders, trying to steady the spinning she felt. Her head lolled back and her eyes closed when she moaned.

"Yes, I love to hear you make those sounds. I can't wait until I'm buried deep in you." He ran his mouth over her skin until he sucked on her nipple lightly, taking it deep into his mouth as his finger did wicked things to her insides.

"Come for me, Lauren. I want to feel you release," he whispered against her heated skin. His finger pumped in and out, slowly gaining speed until her nails dug into his shoulders and she screamed out his name.

She felt as if she were falling backwards. Opening her eyes, she realized Chase was laying her down on the bed from their kneeling position. He quickly pulled her bottoms all the way off, then came over her as his thighs spread her legs wider. She watched as he leaned over and took a condom from the table and ripped the package opened. She'd never seen one before and she couldn't help but wonder how that small disk was going to fit over the length of him.

Then he rolled it on like an expert, and she smiled as he pulled her legs up closer to him. "Hang on to me," he said, then leaned in and started kissing her again. She was so lost in what his mouth was doing to her that when he slid in, she forgot that it was meant to hurt at first. Everything felt so good and when he did quickly breach her maidenhead, she barely felt anything except pleasure.

Her hands gripped his hips, helping him move more quickly. With each thrust, her breath hitched. Her eyes flew open as she watched his face hovering over hers.

His brown eyes seemed to sparkle in the candlelight, and he had a slight smile on his lips until she grabbed his head and pulled him back to her lips.

"You feel so good," she moaned into his ear.

"Oh, god," he said, then his motions changed. He took her left leg and hiked it higher next to his chest. His thrusts grew stronger and longer until she too closed her eyes and was lost in the motion.

When he reached down and placed a fingertip

on the sensitive skin between them, lights exploded behind her eyes and she cried out his name just as he stilled above her.

He leaned down and placed a soft kiss on her lips and said her name before crushing her with his full weight.

Lauren woke several hours later. Chase had moved to the side and had tucked her into his body. There was a thick blanket over them and she realized she was itching like crazy. Tossing the blanket off, she wished for a light to see why she couldn't stop itching.

"Oh, god," she said, causing Chase to jolt from the bed.

"What?" It was dark, but she heard him bang into something. "Son of a..." Then she heard him walking slowly towards the light switch. The dim light flooded the room and she squealed.

Large red welts covered her body and she couldn't stop itching.

"What the hell?" He rushed over to her.

"Wool." She pointed to the blanket. "I'm allergic to that thing. That's why it was out here in the first place." She continued to scratch.

"Don't. Scratching only makes it worse." He took her wrists and pulled them away from her body.

"Help me. It itches so bad. I need a shower. I

need my lotion." She used her chin to scratch her shoulder. "I need to scratch." She tried to tug her hands free as he laughed at her.

"It's not that bad." When she glared at him, he laughed more. "Well, it's not. I've seen worse. I guess you can't go prancing around like this. If I let your hands lose, will you promise me you won't scratch?"

"I make no promises." She glared at him and tugged on her wrists.

"Fine." He leaned down and picked her up and started walking towards the door, her wrists still trapped in his other hand.

"Wait, Chase. What are you doing?" she cried, trying to break free of his hold.

"Well, since you won't stop scratching, I guess I'll just have to carry you to the house like this." She stilled and looked down at them. They were both as they'd come into the world, completely naked. She thought of what her sisters would think if he walked into the house. Naked. Carrying her. Naked.

"Fine, I promise," she said between gritted teeth.

He nodded and set her down, still holding her wrists. Putting her chin up, she waited until he released her. Her hands went to her sides and it took all her control not to start scratching.

She closed her eyes and thought about last night

and what they'd done, to keep her mind off the itching. She could hear him rummaging around, then finally her shirt was deposited over her head.

"Here, step into these." She opened her eyes and held onto his shoulders as she stepped into her PJ bottoms. He was completely dressed, down to his boots. When she'd gotten the bottoms on, he picked her back up.

"We'll worry about the rest later. Let's get you into a bath with some salts first." He hit the light switch with his elbow and shut the door with his foot as they left the shelter.

The sun was just coming up when he marched into the kitchen, carrying her. Thankfully, no one was awake yet.

"Where's your room?" He took the stairs two at a time.

"Last door on the left," she whispered. "Hurry."

Her room was the largest in the house and had been her parents' room. It had taken her almost five years to finally move into it. Every time she thought about moving in, she would back down. It wasn't until Alex started moving her things into the room that she had finally put her foot down and moved her things in. Alex had quickly and quietly moved into Lauren's old room without complaint. Haley was still in her childhood bedroom and, to Lauren's knowledge, was content.

Chase set her down and when she opened her

eyes, she realized she was in the bathroom. He was leaning over the tub, putting the stopper in. Then he switched on the water, testing the warmth.

"It takes a few minutes to get warm," she said.

"Utt, utt," he said, looking over at her. She hadn't realized she had started scratching again. Her hands fell to her sides and she tried to think of anything that would take her mind off the itching.

"Do you have any Epsom salt?"

She nodded and pointed to the sink, then tried to focus on something else. Looking around the large bathroom, she thought of all the things she'd like to fix once she could afford it. The old claw bathtub was still in great condition. The stand-alone shower looked new with fresh tile and faucets. But the sink and toilet had to go. She hated the seventies green. Maybe some new paint throughout the entire place?

"Here." He took her hands and pulled her to her feet. "Let's get you into the tub." He pulled her shirt over her head and gasped when he saw the large white and red welts covering her skin.

"I know. It sucks, huh?" She looked down at herself and frowned. The welts were a lot bigger now.

"It's okay, we'll get you all fixed up." He helped her pull off her bottoms and then walked her over to the tub.

The hot water had almost steamed the room

completely. She knew that her sisters wouldn't have hot water for at least a few hours. But then again, they probably wouldn't be up until the water heater was full again. She knew Alex didn't work on Fridays and Haley was hardly ever up this early, but still she tried not to make too much noise as she slid into the warm bath.

It took a few seconds for the salts to start soothing the itch that covered every inch of her body. Finally feeling better, she rested her head back against the ledge and sighed with relief. Chase sat next to her, watching. He leaned over and took a washcloth from the low shelf and dipped it into the warm water, then started running it gently over her skin.

"This should start making your welts go down." He frowned as he looked at her skin. It wasn't the first time that blanket or another one like it had caused her grief. The first time she remembered seeing her skin welt up was when she was five. Her father had found her fast asleep in the barn, cuddled up to the new colt she'd watched being born earlier that day. Her father had grabbed a horse blanket and had tried to keep her warm as she slept in the soft hay. She'd woken a few hours later, her hands and arms covered with the welts. She'd cried so hard and had associated the pain with sleeping in the hay. It had taken her years to even touch hay after that. Finally, they had found out what had caused the welts when she'd gone on a picnic with her sisters. Alex had spread out a large horse blanket and they'd lain on it wearing nothing but their swimsuits in the warm spring sun. Lauren had started itching five minutes later and had rushed home completely covered in sores.

Looking down at her body, she realized this was the worst it had ever been. She must have lain under that blanket, asleep in glorious bliss, for hours. Looking down at her hands, she realized they were two times their regular size.

"Okay, I didn't want to freak you out," he said, still moving the washcloth over her arms. "But I think we need to get you down to the clinic." He stood up and grabbed her large white robe. "The swelling is getting worse."

She shook her head. "I have some pills. In the medicine cabinet." She leaned her head back and listed to him rifling around her medicine cabinet.

"Here." When she opened her eyes he was leaning down, a small pink pill and a glass of water in his hands a glass of water.

After she swallowed the pill, there was a knock on the bathroom door.

Lauren quickly put her fingers to her lips, signaling Chase to be quiet. "What?" she called out.

"You used all the hot water," Alex complained from the other side of the locked door.

"I'm sorry. I needed a bath." She closed her eyes and groaned when her sister started in on a long line of complaints. It was an old routine that they'd been through hundreds of times. She was shocked when she heard the door open, and her sister's complaints quickly dropped off.

"It's my fault," Chase said, quickly. "I covered her with the blanket she's allergic to in the shelter." He motioned towards her. "She's covered in welts."

"Oh!" Alex rushed in and looked down at her sister's red swollen skin. "Lauren! I'm so sorry. It's my fault, really." She turned towards Chase. "I'm the one that didn't want to toss that blanket out. Sentimental reasons. Are you alright?"

Lauren nodded her head and wished she was anywhere but lying naked in front of Chase and her sister at the moment.

"I'm marching down there right now and getting rid of that old thing." Her sister quickly left the room.

Chase locked the door behind her and leaned back against the door.

"Why?" She looked at him. "Why did you do that?"

He smiled a little. "It was better than listening to her complain for a few hours." He started walking towards her, removing his shirt as he went. She couldn't stop herself from enjoying the slow striptease he did as he walked towards her. By the time he reached the edge of the tub, he was standing in front of her completely and gloriously naked.

"Scoot up." He motioned towards the head of the tub.

She chuckled. "There isn't enough room in this thing for two."

"Wanna bet?" He smiled and her mouth went dry.

She scooted up and watched him grab the edge of the tub and slowly lower himself in the water. "Here, put your legs over mine." It took them a few minutes to get settled, during which time Lauren giggled more than she had in years. Finally, they settled with her legs over his as they faced each other. He picked up the washcloth again and dumped some of her shampoo into it and his hands, then began to slowly rub her skin.

The extra-strength Benadryl had started working and her head was feeling a little fuzzy. She leaned back as he washed her itchy skin.

"Feeling better?" His voice was low.

"Mmmm." She nodded, then dropped her head back against the high edge.

He took his time, running the cloth slowly over every inch of her. She knew he was enjoying it as much as she was and by the time he stood up, he could see that her skin was starting to go back to its normal size and color again.

"Here." He handed her a towel after wrapping one around his hips. "I'll make you some breakfast. You need to rest a little." He gathered her up after she stood, then carried her to her bed and laid her down gently.

"You don't have to." She leaned back against her soft pillows and yawned.

"You really needed some food in your stomach before you took the pill. I'll just make you some toast and eggs."

"Hmm, okay." She turned and snuggled into her soft comforter as he walked out her door wrapped in nothing but her white cotton robe.

Chapter Twelve

Chase stood at the stove cooking eggs, Dingo at his feet, as he watched the sun rise in the large window. He was starting to feel more frustrated at Lauren, especially after looking around her bathroom, bedroom, and kitchen. He wanted to shake her for not doing some basic minor fixes to the place over the years. At the top of his list was a new water heater, then a new refrigerator and stove. He wanted to kick the old thing he was trying to cook on now. Half the burner didn't work and when it did, if he didn't watch it closely, it burned the eggs. Even her toaster needed to be replaced.

He didn't want to march in here and start complaining about how she'd been living, but there were some things that just couldn't be avoided. The stove was a fire hazard. He cringed to think of what the water heater or the furnace was like.

When he carried the eggs and toast up to her, he paused just inside her door. Her skin was back to its normal soft creamy color. The welts were all but gone as he looked over the rest of her. Setting the plate down, he crawled into the bed behind her and decided to shut down for a while.

When he woke a few hours later, he looked up into Haley's smiling face as she sat on the end of the bed looking between him and Lauren.

"Hey." He reached up and rubbed his eyes and stretched his arms over his head. Lauren shifted next to him and snuggled into his chest as Haley's smile got bigger.

"Hey, yourself," she said loud enough that Lauren jolted upward. He watched in humor as Lauren groaned and closed her eyes and leaned her head back against the headboard.

"Does anyone in this house know how to knock?" Lauren groaned and tried to cover herself with the blanket.

"I knocked," Haley said as she scooted closer to her sister. "So, you and Chase, huh?"

Chase chuckled at Lauren's response. She pulled the blankets back and looked at her sister. "Go away now and I may let you live."

"Fine, fine. We'll talk later," she said as she started walking towards the door.

"Fine," Lauren said and lay back.

"Oh, I wasn't talking to you. I was talking to Chase." Haley smiled and shut the door behind her as Chase laughed.

He leaned down and pulled Lauren closer to him. The soft feel of her, the scent of her shampoo, sent little waves of awareness throughout his entire system.

"Hmm, this feels nice." She snuggled her back against him and he was very aware that under the blankets she was completely naked. "I'm sorry about my nosy sisters."

He chuckled. "I'll forgive them, especially since Haley made sure to lock the door when she left."

Lauren chuckled and then moaned as he started running his lips over the soft skin just under her ears. "You taste so wonderful." He listened to her breath catch. Then she completely shocked him by turning over and pulling the blankets off of them both. He quite literally lost every thought in his head as he looked at her soft perfect skin.

She couldn't help it, she wanted more of him, and she wasn't opposed to taking what she wanted.

Pulling herself up, she straddled his narrow hips and was happily surprised when she felt his hardness press against the insides of her thighs. His eyes went directly to her breast and she ran her hands over her skin as she watched his eyes heat with desire. Then she leaned down and ran her hands slowly over his chest, making sure to spend time on each of his flat nipples. His eyes watched hers and she could feel his muscles bunch under her exploration. She scooted further down on his hips as she ran her fingers lower over his abdomen, finally wrapping her hand around his erection. He groaned and closed his eyes as she began to explore the length and girth of him.

It impressed her that he could be so hard while his skin was feather soft. She leaned down and kissed his hips as she continued to let her fingers explore him. His hands went to her hair, holding her, pushing her away, she didn't know. The salty taste of him sent shivers down her spine until finally she leaned over and took his length into her mouth. Enjoying the sounds he made and the way his hips jolted when she stroked her mouth up and down him, she decided this form of pleasure could easily entertain them both.

"Enough," he groaned and put his hands under her arms, hauling her up until she was straddling his hips again. "You'll pay for that." He smiled, then leaned up and took her nipple into his mouth. His hands ran over every inch of her, spreading goose bumps on her exposed skin.

She didn't realize she had started moving her hips, grinding him, until his hands started helping her move over him, his fingers biting into her soft skin slightly. The more he pushed her, the more she wanted to move faster.

"Lauren, give me a second." He sat up a little and reached for his jeans. She watched as he pulled a condom from his pocket.

She felt a wave of excitement run through her as she reached out and took the small package from him. Her eyes were glued to his as she opened it and took the condom in her fingertips. She stared at it for a second, and then slowly slid it onto him.

His fingers flexed on her hips like she'd shocked him. "Did I hurt you?"

He smiled and shook his head. "No, but you're driving me crazy."

She smiled a little. "I like knowing I can do that to you. That I do this to you." She took him into her hand and moved up and down slowly as his eyes closed and his head rested back on the bed.

Then she got onto her knees and hovered just above him, pausing as she adjusted their positions. Slowly she started moving down onto him as his fingers dug into her soft hips. When she was fully impaled, she started moving. The pleasure was building and with it, her speed grew. Leaning down, she started placing kisses along his collarbone as his hands ran through her hair softly.

With each stroke, her heart beat harder in her chest and her breath hitched and, slowly, everything else faded from her mind except the feeling of him deep inside her. His groans of delight matched her own. Sweat made their skin glisten in the light streaming in from her laced curtains. Finally, he leaned up and took her mouth with his and muffled her screams of delight as his body tensed with his own release.

It took a while for Lauren to start feeling her body again. When she finally did, she realized she was spread out on top of Chase and that she needed another shower.

"What do you say to a cold shower and some lunch?" She leaned up and looked into his face. For some reason, she was totally refreshed and feeling very energetic.

He smiled up at her. "I made you breakfast." He nodded to the plate on her nightstand. Then he frowned. "You need a new stove."

She got up and took a bite of the cold toast. "I know. It's on my list." She took the toast into the bathroom with her and started running the water. She didn't know why she bothered, but she turned the hot water knob as well, just in case her sisters had left anything in the water tank.

Chase walked in and leaned against the door jam. "This whole place could use a makeover."

She didn't want to spoil her good mood, so instead of responding, she walked into the shower and gasped at the coldness. Even though it was probably already in the nineties outside, that didn't mean she wanted a freezing cold shower first thing in the morning. Lathering up her hair, she watched as Chase opened the shower doors and stepped in.

"At least the shower is bigger than the tub." He took a handful of shampoo and started helping her wash her hair.

"Yes, I've always liked this shower." She looked at the large glass enclosure. Its two large glass walls made it feel really open. The tile had been new a few years before her father had passed away and still shined.

"Overall, the place has good bones. I'm not saying it needs a total remake, just a few things here and there. That stove is a death trap. You know, I was in Tyler a few days back. I noticed an appliance store just as..."

"No." She turned and glared at him. "We are not having this discussion." She tried to quickly rinse her hair, but he pulled her into his arms.

"Listen, it's natural that I want to make sure you and your sisters are safe. I'm not butting in. Besides, it's your money."

She would have jerked out of his arms, but the floor was very slippery and she didn't want to land on her butt. "No." She looked up at him and blinked the water from her eyes. "It's not. The money is yours." She would have crossed her arms over her chest, but didn't think it would give the same feeling as it did when she was fully clothed.

He kissed her on the forehead and chuckled. "Okay, at least we agree on that, then. So, you agree that the money you've put in our joint account is mine to do with what I want."

"Yes," she sighed with relief, "completely yours."

"Good." He started running his hands up and down her wet skin and she forgot all about their small argument.

After their shower and a sandwich lunch on the front porch, they saddled the horses and rode out to help the ranch hands with branding the new stock of cattle that had been brought in from the hills. It was getting closer to auction time and Jimmy and the hands were busy separating which animals would go to auction and which ones would be staying on. It was a hot and messy job filled with hours out in the sun, and by the time they rode back to the barn, both of them were covered in dust and were in desperate need of another shower.

Lauren and Dingo walked into the kitchen together. She sat on the chair, resting her head on the cool table as Dingo lay down on her bed by the back door. Haley was moving around in the kitchen, cooking dinner. Every muscle on Lauren's body was sore, she smelled like cow, and probably looked like she felt.

Chase walked in the back door a few minutes later, smiling. "Smells good in here." He walked over and placed a light kiss on Haley's cheek. Haley swatted his hand away from the bowl of fruit she'd been mixing for fruit salad. "If you go wash up, you're welcome to have some. I've made enough."

"Wish I could, but I've got to head into town," he said as he leaned against the counter.

Lauren felt her heart drop a little. She had expected him to stick around, and had hoped that she wasn't showing her disappointment on her face. She didn't know what to expect, and the more she thought about it, the more she realized she didn't know what he expected. Did he think he was going to move into the main house? Into her bedroom? Did she want him to?

"Hot date?" Haley looked at him as he chuckled and shook his head.

"Dinner with my dad. It's a standing Friday night thing." He looked over at her. "I thought you might want to join me?"

Her chin dropped a little so she quickly closed it. "No, I'll pass tonight."

He shrugged his shoulders. "No problem. I'll just head out and clean up." He walked over to her and leaned over. "Standing offer. Just let me know and dad will add another place setting." He quickly kissed her, lingering on her lips for a few seconds. "I'll see you later." He stood up and nodded to Haley, then walked out.

Less than two seconds later, Haley turned on her, salad tongs in hand. "Okay, spill." She leaned back against the counter.

"What?" She tried to look innocent.

"Lauren Marie West, you were in bed with Chase and you are going to tell me everything."

Her eyebrows shot up. No one had used that tone with her since her mother had been alive. Haley stood by the stove, apron on, the smell of cooking filling the air, and all Lauren could think about was how much Haley reminded her of their mother. Tears started to fill her eyes and in the next second, Haley was by her side.

"Was it that bad?"

She shook her head. "You just reminded me of mom for a second."

"Really?" Haley was the only sister that didn't have any memories of their mother. Lauren nodded her head and hugged her sister.

"You remind me the most of her. She had lighter hair, but you move a lot like she did."

Haley smiled. "So, you and Chase, huh?"

Lauren sighed. "Yeah, I guess so."

"What?" Haley stood up and got back to work. "Don't you want Chase to hang around?"

"I don't know. I don't have time to have a relationship."

Haley turned on her, a startled look on her face. "This wasn't a one night stand was it?"

Lauren laughed. "With Chase? Chase doesn't do anything once." When she realized what she'd said, she blushed a little.

Haley laughed and turned back around. "Good. I'd hate to have to sic Alex on him."

An hour later, Chase walked into his father's place with Buddy in his arms and stopped cold when he saw his father's arms wrapped around a tall blonde woman.

"Oh, excuse me." He turned to go, but his father turned around.

"Don't be silly, boy. Come over here and meet my new gal. Charlotte, this is my boy I've been telling you all about."

Chase set Buddy down and he quickly disappeared, no doubt looking for his father's dog to play with. Chase shook Charlotte's hand and took in the woman's appearance. She was around his father's age, but a little shorter and a whole lot skinnier. Her clothes were neatly pressed and she looked like she'd taken great care in her appearance. His father had dated in the past, but no one had ever stuck around long. Somehow, he thought this time would be different. He could see it in his father's eyes.

"How do you do?"

"Oh, just fine. I told Johnathan that he should warn you I'd be coming along tonight." She shook his hand in a firm but friendly handshake. His opinion of her tripled with the warmth he felt in her hands and the humor he saw in her eyes. Chase always disliked women who shook hands like they were so fragile they couldn't muster enough energy to hold onto someone's hand.

"Don't worry about it. I like surprises." He took her arm and steered her towards the dining room. "Well, since my father has left out mentioning you, ever"—he looked over his shoulder at his dad, who immediately looked away—"I'd love for you to fill me in on all the details of how and when you two met." Charlotte smiled and chuckled a little.

An hour later, Chase was laughing so hard, he could hardly contain himself. Charlotte had told him the story of how she'd met him at the medical clinic. She was a physical therapist assigned to her father. Needless to say, his dad hadn't wanted to listen to her but, in the end, she'd whipped him into shape.

"Damned if I don't like this one, Dad." He slapped his father on the shoulder. "If you don't keep her, I think I'll take a shot at her myself." He watched a slow smile cross his father's face.

"You're too late, son. I called dibs on her first."

Charlotte smiled and reached across the table and took his father's hand.

"So, tell me all about this girl you're living with. Lauren was her name, right Johnathan?" Chase started coughing on the mouthful of water he'd just drunk. When he finally cleared his throat, he said. "I'm not living with her, per se. I'm staying in one of her ranch hand's houses."

"Sure he is." He watched his father's eyes fill with humor.

"Oh," she chuckled, "I was led to believe—"

"Yes," he broke in, "I can guess what you were told." He looked towards his father, who had quickly looked away again, a slight smile on his face.

On the drive home, he thought about his situation. Why was he staying in a small, lonely house out in the fields when what he wanted was less than a mile away? By the time he drove up to the ranch, he couldn't shake the question from his mind. He'd seen the look of disappointment in Lauren's eyes when he'd said he couldn't stay for dinner. The fact that she'd wanted him to stay had given him hope. Did that mean she wanted him to stay the night, as well? Now that both her sisters knew they'd spent the night together, why would they hide their relationship? He reached the turn off towards his place, but at the last moment decided to head straight towards the big house instead.

Parking in front of the garage, he picked up Buddy and tucked the sleeping dog under his arm. Looking up towards the house, he saw Lauren's light on and decided to avoid the possibility of running into her sisters in the kitchen. There was a small deck on the second floor. The stairs were a little rickety, but he made his way up the stairs and knocked lightly on her locked window. It took a few times, but finally her curtains were thrown back and she looked at him from the other side of the glass.

She reached down and started to open her window, but it didn't budge. He put Buddy down on a cushioned chair a few feet away, then walked over and started helping her lift the window. In the end, it took a few more tries and both of them to yank the old window open enough that he could step in. He walked over and gathered the sleeping dog and stepped through.

"That's a hazard," he said, setting Buddy down on a lounge chair that sat in front of her other window. "What if there had been a fire? There is no way you would have been able to get out by yourself." He turned and started looking at the old wood and sill. There was an inch of paint caked around the glass. It needed to be scraped off. Better yet, all the windows should be completely replaced.

"I would have broken the glass," she said from behind him. He looked over his shoulder at her. She stood with her arms crossed over her chest. Little black shorts hugged her hips and a small black tank top showed her every curve. He forgot about the window and slowly walked towards her, his mind blanked of everything but her. All he could think of was getting his hands on her soft skin.

"What are you doing here?" She was oblivious to his mood. Well, he would just have to show her that he intended to spend the rest of his nights in her bed.

Jill Sanders

Chapter Thirteen

Chase stood in front of her, a funny look on his face. When he started coming towards her, heat flooded her body. It may have taken her brain a few seconds more to understand what his intentions were, but her body had picked up on it before her mind had.

By the time he'd gathered her up in his arms, she was back in sync and wrapped her arms and legs around him as he carried her a few steps to her bed. When she hit the mattress with a slight bounce, she had no time to recover before he was covering her, his mouth on hers, spreading warmth and heat to every inch of her. When had she lost control?

Her fingers dug into his hair as she tried to pull him closer. She didn't remember him removing her clothes or her pulling his off in return. He paused briefly to put on a rubber, but kept kissing her and building something deep inside her as he protected them. All that she could focus on was the feel of his skin next to hers, the feel of his hands on her, pleasing and pushing her to the very edge.

His calloused hands gripped her hips as he spread her legs wider with his knees. When he slid into her, she felt like something had been missing all day, and realized it had been this. Simply him.

His every movement made time stretch, made every breath she took seem like it was for him. How could he have changed her so much with just a kiss? He trailed his hot mouth down the column of her neck and sent shivers through her entire body. She felt like she couldn't get close enough, pulling her arms around him and wrapping her legs around his narrow hips as he moved above her.

"Faster, Chase. I can't..." She ended on a moan as his lips closed around her nipple and he sucked gently on the peaked skin. His tongue twirled around her heated skin, torturing her with his patience. How could he be in such control? Feeling a little frustrated that his desire wasn't matching hers, she pushed him up and over until finally she was looking down at his smiling face.

"My turn." She dipped her head down and started running her tongue over his chest and flat nipples. His hands went into her hair, holding it back so she could explore every muscle, every inch of his glorious chest as she moved her hips and sent him deeper. She quickened her motion and was pleased when he groaned and grabbed her hips, helping her move.

Then, just when she thought she couldn't stand it anymore, she leaned back and looked down at him. His deep eyes were locked onto her own, a slight smile on his lips as he watched her move over him. Closing her eyes, she held that image as her body convulsed around his.

Then she was being gently moved as he reversed their positions again. He took her leg and pulled it close to his side, pulling her leg over his arm. When she looked up, his smile had deepened, and there was a fierce look of determination and unmistakable lust in his eyes.

"Now, it's my turn." His hips started moving quicker, his thrusts grew longer and deeper until she was lost to the motion. He pinched her nipple between two fingers gently and she moaned moaning again. "I love the sounds you make as I'm pleasing you,"

he said against her skin. She reached up and held onto his arms as he took complete control. She watched his face and could tell he was building up to his release. Pulling him down towards her, she placed a soft kiss on his lips as every muscle in his body tensed with pleasure.

Lauren lay there and listened to his heartbeat slow down. His breathing had leveled out and she could feel the light sheen of perspiration on his skin. She'd never felt so alive, and even though he was crushing her with his weight, she didn't want this moment to end.

"I hope you don't mind us crashing here," he said, then placed a soft kiss on her shoulder.

"Hmm, anytime." She smiled up at the ceiling.

"Good, because I don't think I could move if the house was on fire." She chuckled.

"Don't. I like it right where you are."

"Hmm, you smell wonderful." He began to place soft kisses on her neck and she was amazed that she could feel him growing inside her again. "On second thought, maybe I can move." She chuckled and was happy he could.

The next morning she woke an hour before sunrise. She had a full day ahead of her. She had to work the morning shift at the diner and then she needed to help her men vaccinate the cattle that were going off to be auctioned. Looking down, she noticed Buddy snuggling with Dingo on the dog bed and sighed. They looked so cute together.

Half an hour later, when she stepped out of the bathroom fully dressed, she saw Chase coming back in through the window with Buddy in his arms. Dingo jumped through the opening, looking totally pleased that there was another way into the house. "He had to go out. You know, you could probably turn that window into a patio door." He set Buddy down and stood looking at her window.

"I've thought about it." She reached down and picked Buddy up and scratched between his ears. "I've got to get going. I have the early shift at Mama's." She hugged the small dog and set him back down next to Dingo, then gave her loyal dog a few pats on the head.

"Okay." He turned and kissed her, then went back to looking at her wall.

"Chase?"

"Hmmm?" He didn't turn around.

"What are your plans for the day?"

"Oh, I have some personal things to take care of." He turned and gave her his full attention. "Why?"

"Well, I was thinking maybe we could have lunch before I ride out and help with the cattle."

"Sounds great. What do you say to eating at my place? I need to get a few things there. Then I have some work that needs to be done."

She thought about it and nodded. "Sounds good. I'll see you there."

When she got to Mama's a little before six, the diner was already packed. She liked working a few hours here and there, because it afforded her the time to catch up with some of the people in town. The extra money in her pocket didn't hurt either. Of course, she'd been depositing that money into their joint account to pay Chase back in hopes of having her freedom someday.

She quickly put her purse in the back and got to work. Shifting around the place—refilling coffee mugs, delivering food, and taking orders—she couldn't stop thinking about her and Chase's relationship. Did she still want her freedom from him? Sure, she now viewed them as being in a relationship, but did that mean she wanted to stay married to him?

By eleven she was ready to leave, and her head hurt from running the question over and over in her mind. She knew she didn't have to make any major decisions just yet, but still, she took her time and deposited her latest check from the diner into the bank.

She was shocked when she found out that Chase had withdrawn a large chunk. She knew she'd told him that he could do whatever he wanted with the money. After all, it was his. But still, there was a part of her that was sad to see the large balance going down for once. It also made her think about the changes in their relationship, the uncertainty of what was to come.

When she drove up to his place, he was setting a large salad bowl on the picnic table. When he looked up and smiled, her mind cleared. By the time she turned off her truck, he was there opening the door for her. He pulled her into a hug and kissed her lightly.

"Hello." She couldn't explain it, but her body

just melted when he looked at her like that.

"Hi. Did you have a good morning at the diner?"

"Yes, fairly uneventful. How was your morning?"

He smiled and tugged her towards the table. "Very productive. I'm starving. I hope you don't mind, but I thought we'd just do a salad and sandwiches."

"Sounds wonderful. I've got to head out soon to help the men." She fanned herself as she sat in the shade; even here it was almost too hot to be comfortable. She had changed from her diner uniform to her jeans, shirt, and boots at the diner. Even though the clothing was hotter than her skirt and blouse, it felt more comfortable.

"Here, have some tea." He poured her a glass. It felt good to just sit in the shade and enjoy a simple meal. By the time her sandwich was gone, the heat no longer bothered her. She was laughing so hard and enjoying her time with Chase so much that when she looked down at her watch, she was shocked at how fast the hour had gone by.

As she drove out to the large barn at the back of the north field, she was already looking forward to seeing him at dinner.

Driving up, she parked next to Jimmy's old truck. The men were on their horses, separating cattle. Jimmy and Larry, another longtime worker, were working in the small stalls, giving immunizations to the cattle. It was a two-person job and she knew just how sore a person would be at the end of the day from doing any part of it.

Getting out of the truck, she wasn't surprised to see Dingo jog up to her. Taking a moment, she bent and pet the loyal dog. When she walked up to Jimmy, he looked a little relieved.

"Good, we could use the extra hand." He stood up and wiped the sweat from his face with a white handkerchief.

"Are we short staffed?" She looked around and counted heads. To her count, three men were missing. She saw Haley out in the mix of men and felt a little proud that her sister could keep up with the hardest of men.

"Yeah, well," Jimmy stepped up to the fence and rested his boot on the bottom rung. "I had to let my nephew go." He tipped his hat back and she got a look at his face. Large black bruises ran down the left side of his face. His left eye was swollen and black.

"What happened?" She stopped right in front of him, grabbing his face with her hands. "Jimmy?"

"Let's just say that a few men will no longer be on the payroll. I'll take some time next week to replace them, but until then"—he motioned towards the large herd of cattle—"we have our hands full. It may take us a few more days to get it all done, but we'll get 'er done." He pulled his hat back down on his head. "If you're ready to help..."

She crawled up and over the fence and got to work.

Chase wiped the sweat from his brow and stood back. "Not a bad job." He looked down at Buddy and Dingo who sat at his feet, both of their tails wagging as they looked up at him. Buddy's head was tilted like he was trying to understand. "I just hope she doesn't skin me alive when she sees this."

Just then he heard a noise behind him. When he spun around, he saw Lauren standing inside the doorway. There was a thick layer of dust covering every inch of her. Her hair had straw and hay sticking out of it. Sweat had streaked down her brow, clearing the dust in long lines down her face. Her jeans and shirt were brown from dirt and she smelled like cow. She'd removed her boots and stood in front of him in her socks.

"What is that?" She pointed behind him.

"Well, it's what we've been working on all day. Do you like it?" He turned and looked at the large French doors that led to the back deck.

She shrugged her shoulders and started to walk

past him towards the bathroom. He caught up with her just as she pulled her dirty shirt off and tossed it into the dirty clothes bucket. He had expected something, some sort of response, but her lack of caring concerned him.

"You aren't mad?" He leaned back against the door and watched her strip off her pants, exposing a small pair of red panties that made his mouth water.

"It's not like I can make you put back my wall." She walked over and flipped on the water, checking the temperature before stripping off the rest of her clothes and stepping in and shutting the glass doors.

He walked over and stood outside the steamy glass, watching her hazy image as she rinsed her body off. He couldn't keep his body from reacting to hers as she did her unintentional erotic show. Quickly removing his clothes, he stepped in behind her. She didn't even open her eyes as he pulled her closer and ran his hands over her slick body.

"Rough day?" He leaned in and placed a kiss on her forehead.

"Hmmm. We're short staffed." She leaned her head against his shoulder.

"Why didn't you call me? I could have helped." He pulled back and looked down at her. It stung a little, knowing that she hadn't thought to ask him for help.

"You said you had things to do. I had no idea one of those things was cutting a huge hole in the side of my house." He could feel the tension leaving her body as she spoke. Her arms hung on his shoulders and her body pressed up tight against his.

He *had* led her to believe he'd be busy all day. Had he known that they needed help in the fields, he would have gladly postponed his surprise. He felt like a fool for spending his day working on something so unimportant when there had been real work that needed to be done. Well, the good thing about him was that he was a quick learner. First thing, he was going to have a talk with Jimmy about giving him a call when he needed help.

For now, all he could do was make sure Lauren felt better. He ran his hands down her body, turned her to face away from him, then took a handful of soap and scrubbed her hair clean of the dust and dirt. She moaned and placed her hands against the tiled walls, trying to steady herself. Once he had rinsed her hair clean, he soaped up his hands and ran them over every inch of her body as she held onto his shoulders. He made sure she was rinsed off, then he shut off the cold water and wrapped her in a large towel, picking her up and carrying her to the bed. She sighed and looked up at him, wrapping her arms around him. "Don't go anywhere."

"Never," he whispered, then followed her down to the soft bed, pulling her close as she snuggled next to him.

Lauren woke several hours later and realized she was alone, except for Buddy who was snuggled deep next to her. The little dog sure did sleep a lot. She tried to move him aside, only to have him snuggle deeper. She chuckled as she sat up and looked around. The bright colors from the sunset were coming in her new French doors. Pulling on a pair of shorts and a tank top, she walked over and looked at the doors. She'd always wanted to put doors there. It's what her father had intended to do years ago when he had built the deck, but he'd never had the chance. Reaching down, she opened it and was surprised how easily the door glided opened. Walking out on the deck, she smiled as Buddy followed her outside. The sun was setting, causing the sky to be filled with a million colors. Sitting down on a cushioned chair, she sighed and enjoyed the quiet moment alone.

Just as the last lights from the sun touched the fields, she heard Chase behind her. "Beautiful, isn't it?"

She turned and saw him leaning against the

door jam, Dingo at his feet.

"Yes. Thank you for the doors." She stood and walked over to him. "They're just what I needed today."

"Really?" He wrapped his arms around her. "Buddy and Dingo thought that you were going to rip a hole in me for putting them in without permission."

"Well, on any other day, they would have been right. But after today," she sighed and looked off towards the fields. "I don't mind."

"Your sister made us dinner. Would you like to go downstairs?"

"Depends." She leaned back and smiled at him.

"On?" He brushed a strand of her hair away from her face.

"Which sister cooked." They both laughed.

Jill Sanders

Chapter Fourteen

$\mathcal{B}$y the noon the next day, Lauren wanted to kill Chase. He had decided to come along and lend a hand helping with the separating and vaccination of the cattle. It wasn't that he was annoying her, it was just that with him around, she found it hard to concentrate on her work.

Since he was a veterinarian, he and Jimmy handled vaccinating the cattle. She had to admit, with him helping, they were flying through the herd at a high rate. She was on Tanner's back, helping herd the cattle to the pen where they would get vaccinated. Haley was on her horse, Olivia, and there were four other riders helping herd the cattle. Every time she looked over at Chase, she would lose track of the cow she'd been herding. It had happened four times now and she was getting really frustrated.

Chase, for his part, hadn't done anything other than working in only a white tank top, faded jeans, dusty brown boots, and his favorite Stetson. He looked like he'd come right off the cover of a magazine. How was anyone supposed to concentrate with him looking like that?

Finally, she gave up and rode over to where he and Jimmy were wrestling a calf, both of them laughing as the small thing tried to kick at them.

Sliding off Tanner's back, she walked over and leaned on the fence. "Need some help, boys?"

Just then, Chase looked over at her and was rewarded with a solid kick to his thigh. He lost his grip of the calf and fell to his knee only to be kicked again in the shoulder.

"Damn it." Jimmy pulled the calf away and swatted its backside, sending it running to its waiting mother. "Are you okay?" Jimmy stood over Chase. Lauren had jumped the fence and was kneeling beside him, asking the same thing.

"Fine, I'm fine." Chase rubbed the two spots, his eyes closed for a moment. "That little guy landed a couple good blows."

She could already see the large bruise forming on his shoulder. Reaching over, she took his arm and moved it slowly. "Does this hurt?"

He smiled. "No, Doc. I'll live."

She glared at him. "Be serious for just one moment, will you? He could have done some irreversible damage."

He smiled even more. "I've been kicked by animals before. I'll be fine." He started to stand only to have her place her hands on his shoulder.

"Let me see your thigh." She started pulling at his pants.

"The hell I will. Not right now, anyway." Chase pulled her hands away from his crotch. Jimmy laughed and took off his hat and walked away.

"Chase, I need to know if he broke anything."

"Only my pride." Chase stood and laughed a little. "It's really all your fault, you know."

"What?" She stood and crossed her arms over her chest. "Why is it my fault?"

He tugged on her braid. "You've been distracting me all day." He pulled her braid a little more, bringing her closer to him. "Do you know how enticing you look herding cattle?" Leaning down, he placed a kiss on her lips, sending shivers down her spine.

"No." She closed her eyes for just a moment. "Actually, I was thinking the same thing. I let four cows get away because of you. I've never lost a cow from my sights before." She pulled back and ran her hands over his shoulders, feeling the welt from the calf's hoof.

"I guess we both have the same problem then." His smile was contagious.

"Looks like." She was about to lean up and kiss him when they heard a groan. Looking over she saw her sister leaning on the horn of her saddle.

"Are you two done yet? We have some real work to do and these cattle aren't going to vaccinate themselves." Laughing, Lauren walked back to Tanner, then looked over her shoulder.

"Put on your shirt, you are very distracting." She smiled. By the time she had gotten settled back on Tanner, she looked over at Chase who had removed his shirt altogether, a mischievous smile on his face.

"If I tell you to put on a coat, will you promise to take off—"

"Ugh!" Haley spun her horse around and bolted to the far field. Lauren and Chase laughed.

"Get back to work. I'm not paying you to stand around looking like a Chippendale dancer."

He frowned up at her. "You're not paying me at all."

She smiled. "Then I'll just have to reward you some other way." She nudged Tanner and took off, following Haley out to the field to gather the next group of cattle.

In the end, it took them a day and a half to finish separating and vaccinating the cattle.

Now it was three days before they had to start moving the herd to Tyler for auction. It would take close to twenty trips to get all of them moved to the auction holding barns.

It was the night before Savannah's charity ball at the Pine's Theater. Lauren and Alex had driven into Tyler to pick out new dresses for the event. Even though she'd let her sister talk her into buying a dress that was out of her price range, she was still excited about attending the event.

Chase had taken to staying with her every night, but tonight he had a few errands to run and told her he wouldn't be back until late. She looked forward to waking up in his arms every morning. He kept spending his money on small things around the house. The other day he'd bought her a new toaster and coffee maker. He'd told her it was because he was staying there and wanted a decent cup of coffee and toast that wasn't burnt, but she knew he was slowly spending her money on things that would make her life easier. She tried to hide her annoyance at it, but enjoyed the good coffee too much to argue with him over it.

She'd been busy in the barn until after sunset and, armed with the financial books, which were tucked under her arm, she stood just inside the barn ready to go in for the night. Haley had just gotten back from a ride on Olivia, and Alex was working late at the diner. Since their little talk, she'd hardly seen her sister around the house. Hopefully, Alex was doing some thinking. Which reminded her that she had some thinking of her own to do. She enjoyed having Chase around, but still felt like he was trying to cross too many lines. Every day she would scold him for trying to butt into the affairs of the ranch or the house. He'd ordered a new tankless water heater for the house, stating that he couldn't stand the thought of cold showers in the winter. She'd caught him looking at new windows on his laptop and had, hopefully, convinced him not to mess with the house. It had been a large fight, but it had ended up with them wrapped around one another a few hours later.

She knew more about the farm than he did and for the most part, he kept his nose out of the running of it. She didn't mind his help out in the fields, but he had better keep out of her books. In the last seven years, she'd learned how to pinch every dime from the books, making her money go farther than even her father had been able to do.

Looking around the barn, even in the dying light, she felt a sense of overwhelming pride knowing that the place was thriving, even in the low economic times. If everything went fine at the auction, she'd be able to pay Chase completely off and could still afford to do some repairs around the house. She knew that Chase was upset that she hadn't used his money to do the repairs, but her priority had been getting herself out from under his debt.

She heard a low sound coming from the back of the barn. Setting the paperwork down, she started walking towards the back, thinking that one of the horses might be sick.

When she got there, she was shocked to see Hewitt leaning against the railing of an empty stall, staring at her.

"What are you doing here?"

"Well, don't you look all pretty tonight." He uncrossed his legs and started walking towards her.

"Hewitt, Jimmy fired you days ago. I expect you to be off my property." She turned and started walking him to the barn door. He reached out and took her arm, holding her in place.

"Now, now. Don't be in such a hurry." He leaned closer and she could smell the alcohol on him.

"Let go." Her voice was low and full of determination. She knew how to handle unwanted advances. She'd worked with plenty of men over the years and Hewitt was no different.

His hand dropped, but he stepped closer. "You're a tease. I could tell from the first time I saw you." His body swayed a little.

"Hewitt, I'm going to give your uncle a call. He'll—"

"The hell with Jimmy. He's nothing to me." The man spat on the ground. Just then, Larry walked in the back door. Larry was a few years older than her, and had been working on the farm since before her father's death. The skinny man looked like he'd walked out of a Marlboro ad. Instead of a cigarette, he always had a toothpick hanging from his lips.

"You okay, Lauren?" He looked between the two of them.

Hewitt dropped his hand and then stormed past her, slamming the door as he left.

Lauren looked at Larry. "Yes, sorry." She started walking towards the front barn door, then turned back towards him. "Tell Jimmy to make sure Hewitt knows that I don't want him on my property anymore." Larry nodded and she walked out the front door.

The next morning she stood in line at the bank, and she cringed inwardly when she saw Savannah walk in behind her.

"Oh, Lauren. Aren't you so excited about tonight?" Savannah was wearing a sparkling pink top that showed off a lot of her busty curves. Even Lauren had a hard time averting her eyes from her friend's cleavage as she chatted about the details of putting the banquet together. The teller line moved slowly, so slowly that it was almost as if Lauren had been thrust into an episode of *The Twilight Zone*, where time all of a sudden stopped. Finally, she walked up to the teller and made her deposit, then turned, hoping to avoid talking with Savannah any more, but her friend stepped out of line and stopped her from exiting the building. Just when she felt like her head would explode, Chase walked in, and a smile spread on his face when he noticed her.

"Well, fancy running into you here." He walked up to them and smiled at her, then at Savannah. Savannah quickly tucked her arm into his, thrusting those ginormous breasts his way. For his part, Chase looked like he was rather enjoying the extra attention. He hadn't pulled away from Savannah and looked like he was rather enjoying the feel of her breast against his arm. A bout of jealousy slammed into her so quick, she clenched her fists.

"I was just telling Lauren about the dress I'll be wearing tonight. Did you know that the Roy Carson Band is going to be there? Roy Carson himself is going to escort me to the ball." She brushed a strand of hair out of her face and looked up at Chase. "Of course it's not the same as having you escort me, Chase. My how you've changed since the last time I saw you." She wrapped her hand around his bicep.

"You know I'd love to take you, Savannah, but Lauren and I are together and I've been looking forward to dancing with my girl again." He smoothly pulled out of Savannah's grip and wrapped his arms around Lauren, placing a steamy kiss on her to top it all off. Jealousy forgotten, she lost herself in the warmth of his embrace and kiss.

When she saw Savannah's pout, she was very thankful Chase had stopped by the bank.

"Well, I didn't know y'all were an item. Don't you two look so cute together." The sarcasm was hidden, but Lauren heard it just the same.

"Yes, we've been together for some time now." Chase looked at Lauren and she could tell he was trying not to laugh at the inside joke.

"Well, I just can't wait to see everyone all dressed up again. Oh, there's Jenny." Savannah waved to someone at the back of the teller line. "I simply must talk to her before tonight." When she turned and walked away, Chase took Lauren's hand in his and walked out of the bank with her.

"Didn't you need to be in the bank for some reason?"

"I am not going back there with her still loose in the building." He chuckled. He stopped her just outside her truck and turned her towards him. "So, tell me really, how jealous were you?"

"I have no idea what you're talking about." She smiled and turned to get into her truck, but was stopped when he turned her back around. His hands were on her shoulders, as he looked down at her.

"Lauren." His chocolate eyes sparkled with humor.

She rolled her eyes. "Oh, fine. It wasn't so much jealousy as it was annoyance that she was rubbing her ginormous chest all over you, and you looked like you were enjoying every moment of it."

He laughed. "Ginormous? Well, I was. I'm a

guy after all, but..." He pulled her closer and wrapped his arms around her. "I can tell you that they didn't do anything for me. Just the thought of having your soft body next to mine does so much for me." He pressed his hips against hers and she could feel his desire. "Just the thought of kissing you makes my mouth water, makes me want to..." He leaned down and took her lips with his. "Lauren, tell me you have some time before we have to go to the ball." He moaned against her skin.

She laughed a little and shook her head. "I have a few errands left to run before I need to start getting ready. If you're good, we might be able to shower together." She looked up at him through her eyelashes.

"It's a date." He kissed her and pulled away to wave to his father, Mr. Holton, and Grant, who were walking towards them. "I've got a few things to pick up, then I'll be home around five." He turned and greeted the men as she quickly ducked into her truck and drove away. She was so wound up, she drove ten miles under the speed limit, just because her imagination wouldn't shut down. By the time she was done running her errands, she thought all it would take was him looking at her for her to explode.

When she got home, she raced through the front door to the sound of the ringing phone and reached it just in time. An hour later, when Chase walked in the front door, she stood in the hallway waiting for him.

He smiled at her and started to pull her close. She yanked out of his arms. "Would you mind telling me why, exactly, you would need a copy of the deed to my ranch?"

Chase pulled back and looked at her. He could tell she was upset. He could feel her vibrating from where he stood. He laughed, which apparently was the wrong thing to do, since she picked up the picture of her and her sisters from the small table and threw it at his head. He easily dodged it and took a step back.

"What business is it of yours to have a copy of the deed to my ranch?" She picked up another small item and started to throw that.

"Lauren, I didn't—" He couldn't say anything else before he was dodging another projectile.

Finally, he rushed over and grabbed her arms, stopping her from picking up anything else.

"It's not for me," he blurted out.

"Oh? Then who's it for? I trusted you. I thought you'd stick to our bargain, but ever since you got back in town, you've done all you can to manipulate me." She tried to push out of his hold.

"How did you find out I requested a copy?"

"Cyndi from the county clerk's office called. She was real worried you wouldn't get the copy in time and just wanted to make sure it had arrived." He could imagine what else Cyndi had said. He'd dated her for a while back in high school and when he'd stopped by the clerk's office, she'd been all too eager to help him out. She'd even written her phone number down on his receipt. He rolled his eyes and tried not to groan.

"Listen, let's head upstairs and I'll explain everything." He took her hand and tried to pull her up the stairs, but she yanked her hand away.

"I want you to leave." She crossed her arms over her chest. "You've broken our agreement and I think it's time that I filed for divorce." She heard a gasp and looked towards the stairs. Both of her sisters stood there, halfway dressed for the night out, their mouths opened wide as they looked down at them.

Lauren's hands dropped to her side and he could see all the blood drain from her face. He rushed over to her and took her arm as she stared at her sisters.

Alex and Haley rushed down the stairs. Alex had large curlers in her hair. Half of Haley's hair was curled, the other half hung straight. "We heard the fighting," Haley explained as she came to stand next to him.

"It's okay. It's about time you two knew anyway." Lauren just looked at him, begging him to be quiet, but it was too late. "We married seven years ago, the day after your father's funeral." He walked Lauren over and sat her down on the couch. She went willingly, almost as if she was in a trance. Her sisters followed and sat opposite them. He continued to hold Lauren's hand as he explained what had happened, why their sister had hidden the biggest secret of her life from them for seven years.

"How could you?" Haley stood up. "We are in this together. We've let you take control on some things, but did you think you had to carry the burden all by yourself?"

Alex stood next to Haley, looking down at them. "I don't know who I'm more disappointed in, you or her." She looked at Chase. "Why would you want to control her like that?" He looked down at their joined hands and knew that he couldn't explain what he'd done seven years ago, even if he wanted to. "And you." She turned and pinned Lauren down with her eyes. "Here you've been going on and on about me making a big mistake by marrying Travis, when you married someone you didn't love seven years ago." Her voice raised a little. "Not only that, you kept it hidden from your sisters. Your only family!" Alex turned and marched out of the room.

He looked up at Haley and could see the hurt in her eyes. "You didn't have to take it all by yourself, you know. We've been right here, all along, waiting for you to ask us for help. But you never did." Haley turned and walked out slowly.

"I'm sorry," Lauren said, finally. She shook her head and he felt a tear fall from her eyes onto his hand.

"Lauren." He turned her towards him. "I'm sorry. This is all my fault." He couldn't explain it, but there was a huge pressure on his chest. "I didn't want the deed for myself. Honest."

She shook her head. "I can't do this right now." She stood and then turned back towards him. "I'm sorry, Chase. I just can't do this right now." Then she turned and ran from the room.

He sat in the living room, Dingo curled up by his feet, feeling like his world was coming to an end. Slowly he made his way back to his place and showered and dressed for the night. He knew that Lauren and her sisters would be at the ball. Even though they were torn, they would show a united front and he wanted to be part of that front, whether he would remain part of their family or not.

When he walked into the Pine's Theater, the place was packed. The old theater sat right off Main Street and had been remodeled several years back. The old movie theater still hosted movies on special occasions, but for the most part was a gathering place for events such as weddings, birthday parties, and special city events.

He was greeted by a waiter and took the offered flute of wine. It took him a while to locate Lauren, but finally he spotted her towards the back corner. Her back was to him as she listened to Savannah, who was wearing a dangerously low-cut red number. When Savannah spotted him, she stopped talking and waved towards him. Lauren turned and he caught his breath. The light green dress matched her eyes perfectly. The silk hugged every curve she had, and he was sure she wore nothing underneath it. She had turquoise around her neck and dangling from her wrist and ears, accenting the color of her eyes even more. His eyes traveled down her flowing skirt to the white, thin-strapped heels that tied around her ankles, adding two inches to her height.

He walked closer, not paying any attention to Savannah as she gushed about how handsome he looked in his tuxedo. Lauren's eyes were focused on his face and he could see her misery written deep in her eyes.

"Can I have a moment?" He took her arm lightly and steered her towards the back hallway.

"Chase, I can't deal with—" He stopped her by pulling out the package that had been tucked under his arm.

"For you." He waited until she took it from him. She looked between him and the silver wrapped package.

"What is it?"

"Open it. I know it's not your birthday for a while, but circumstances being what they are..." He looked down at the package and waited.

She took her time opening the wrapping. He didn't know if she was afraid she'd ruin it or if she was just unsure of what she'd find.

Finally, when the frame was exposed, she looked down at the glass. Her dark hair fell lightly over her eyes so that he couldn't read what was there. Reaching up, he pulled her hair back behind her ear. She looked up at him, tears in her eyes.

"This is why you requested a copy?" she asked as a tear slid down her cheek.

He nodded, unable to say anything. He looked down at his handy work. An old black and white image of her parents sat at the top next to an image of her grandparents that Haley had found for him. An image of her and her sisters sat below it and the copy of the deed sat behind them all, etched in the silver photo mat with Saddleback Ranch's logo above them all.

"It's beautiful." She held the large frame close to her chest as she looked at him. "I'm sorry." She reached up and wiped a tear from her eyes.

"Don't be. Listen, I'm not proud of the decisions I've made, of how I handled things seven years ago." He took the frame from her and set it on the table beside him. Taking her hands in his, he pulled her closer. "I never thought about you, about what you wanted. Only what I wanted."

"I don't understand." She shook her head, sending her earrings bobbing.

"Lauren, I wanted you back then as much as I want you now. I was young and thought the best way to ensure that you wouldn't run off and marry the first man you met was to tie you to me. I knew I had to leave, to go to college, but I wanted to stay here instead. I wanted to be with you and I didn't even have the balls to tell you back then." He sighed. "The sad part is that it's taken me this long to tell you. I want to be with you. I want to stay married to you. To be your real husband, to go to sleep holding you, wake up with you in my arms. I want to spend every day making you smile." He smiled a little as she looked at him like he was crazy. "To help out, take some of the burden from the ranch. I didn't want you to pay me back because I was afraid that if you did, you'd break your ties with me. Now I want nothing more than to spend the rest of my life with you."

"Chase…" She pulled back a little. "I don't know what to say."

Just then the music got louder, and Savannah came and pulled on Lauren's hand. "Lauren, Roy's on. Come on." Her friend pulled her back into the auditorium.

He stood there, looking at her as she retreated.

Then he followed and watched from the doorway as she stood there with her friend as Roy belted out his latest hit. He never removed his eyes from her, even when Grant walked over and started talking to him.

Jill Sanders

Chapter Fifteen

Lauren was dying to get out of the theater. Savannah kept her arm tight in her hands, keeping her in place. Finally, a few songs into Roy's set, the music slowed and Savannah was asked to dance by Grant. Lauren turned to exit, but when she turned she bumped into Chase's chest. Looking up, she saw determination in his eyes. Without saying a word, he put his hand on her back, pulling her close as he took her hand in his.

They started moving across the floor slowly as other couples swirled around them faster. His eyes never left hers as they glided across the floor. She hadn't realized he'd danced them towards the side doors, but when the cool air hit her shoulders, she jolted awake and was freed from the trance of his eyes.

Dropping her hand, she stepped back and

looked around. There was a small patio enclosed by iron fencing. White lights hung on a string overhead that went from tree to tree along the patio. No one else was outside as she walked to lean on the iron fence.

His warm hand came to her shoulder, turning her towards him.

"Talk to me. Tell me I'm not alone in the way I feel."

She shook her head. "No, you're not alone. I just don't...I can't..." She sighed.

"You can. You heard what your sisters said. You've shouldered the burden long enough. Let someone else help you out. I'm here. They're here for you as well." He pulled her closer and when he leaned down and placed a kiss on her lips, she felt something inside her shift.

How had she denied herself for so long? Why hadn't she seen it sooner? She was in love and it was the farthest thing from what she wanted. She needed time to think. Time to sort out what this meant for her and more important, the ranch.

"Chase..." She looked up into his eyes. "I need some time. I need to understand everything."

He kept her gaze for a moment, then sighed and rested his forehead on hers. "I understand. Just don't take too long, Lauren." He pulled back and smiled down at her. "Let's go back in and enjoy the rest of the evening, shall we?"

When she nodded her head, his smile grew. "Have I told you how beautiful you look tonight?"

She shook her head, and smiled a little.

When they walked back in, the floor was full of people jumping and dancing to the loud music. Lauren lost herself in the beat and let her worries float away with every soft song. By the end of the evening, her feet hurt, her head was dull from the wine and champagne, and she was still no closer to understanding what she wanted out of a relationship with Chase.

Early the next morning, she decided an overnight trip to the cabin would help clear her mind. She didn't want to face her sisters just yet, so she decided to sneak out her new French doors. She knew she was being a coward, but she needed this time to do some serious thinking. Since she had a new lock she wanted to put on the door and a few other items that had needed replacing at the cabin since the break in, she packed a larger bag than normal, which meant Dingo would have to stay behind since she wouldn't be able to ride up with her on Tanner's back.

"Sorry, girl. It's just this once. I promise you a big juicy steak when I get back." Dingo sat and dropped her head, appearing to understand the situation as Lauren shut the glass doors behind her, leaving her best friend behind.

The long ride up to the hills helped clear her mind and she made it to the halfway point by noon. Sitting under the tree that she and Chase had sat under a few weeks back, she leaned against the trunk and thought about her future.

It wasn't that she was opposed to being married, she just didn't know if Chase was the right person. She'd always dreamed of having a relationship like her folks had. They'd been quite the team. Her father had taken care of everything around the house, everything except the kitchen. That had been her mother's domain. They had always laughed and enjoyed each other so much and she knew that when her mother died, her father never really recovered from the loss.

She always like to list out the pros and cons of every major decision she had before her, a little trick she learned shortly after signing the marriage license seven years ago.

She started with the cons. Staying married to Chase would mean giving up some of her freedom and her responsibilities around the ranch. Living in a house with two sisters and a husband would get tiring. The old place was big, but not big enough for the four of them for too long.

She couldn't think of any others, so she started listing out the positives. Chase had always been there in her life. She couldn't remember a time when he or his father had been around the farm. She'd grown up with him being a best friend in school. Would he make a great husband? He seemed to want to take care of her and the ranch.

Not to mention he got along great with her sisters. She knew that the physical relationship with him was great, but she didn't really have much to compare it to. It was a nice thought, having someone else there to shoulder some of the burden with the ranch, someone to help make major decisions, to be there to talk to when things got rough.

She sighed and stood up, dusting off her pants. She was picking up her water bottle when she heard the gun shot. She jolted up and automatically reached for her gun. Looking around, she gauged that the shot was less than a mile east of her position.

She doubted any of her men were up this far, since most of the cattle were down in the valley. Rushing over to Tanner, she decided a quick scout around couldn't hurt.

Tanner danced around a little as she put her foot into the stirrup; she didn't hear a sound until she was flying through the air. Lauren heard a loud shot as a bullet passed right by Tanner's ears and landed in the tree that Lauren had been sitting under. She tried to hold onto Tanner's reins, but the horse went up on his hind legs, causing her ankle to twist in the stirrup. For a moment she thought she could get him under control, but he bolted when another shot landed right at his feet. Her foot popped out of the stirrup and she lost hold of the reins as she was thrown back several feet. She landed on her back as her head connected with a large rock and then everything went dark.

Alex was tired of being treated like she was a trophy. Maybe Lauren was right about Travis. After their fight last night at the ball, she just didn't want anyone else to tell her what to do or how to act again. To top it all off, she was having serious doubts that his relationship with Savannah had been a one-time thing.

Alex and Travis had broken it off several times in the past, but nothing as long as the whole month they'd been apart last winter. He'd told her immediately when they'd gotten back together about the one night he'd gotten drunk and stayed with Savannah. But after the way he'd hung on her last night at the ball, she worried that it went beyond a one-time thing.

It was bad enough that Alex couldn't stand the woman, but to be slapped in the face with the knowledge that her fiancé had slept with the viper had almost been too much to bear.

Then her mind turned to Lauren and the hurt tripled. How could her sister have kept such a huge secret from them? Finding out that her sister had gotten married without telling her was hard, and the fact that she'd kept it from her for seven years made it harder.

It wasn't as if she and Haley didn't do their fair share around the ranch. Alex only worked three or four days a week at the diner, and even then she gave up half her pay to her sister to help pay for the bills. She helped out plenty with the animals and was always there to herd the cattle at auction time.

Haley did her part, as well. The girl had missed a great opportunity to go to college down south. Instead, she'd chosen to stay here and help out with the ranch, giving up her dream of becoming a veterinarian altogether so the financial burden wouldn't be too much for her sisters.

Maybe she should leave town? Now that she knew Lauren and Chase were married, she could break off her engagement to Travis, head into the city and...what?

She leaned back on the front porch and sighed as she watched the sun setting. Just then she saw Chase's truck turn into the driveway. She smiled and waved as he pulled to a stop in front of the house.

"Hey, is your sister around?" He stepped onto the porch.

"You mean your wife?" She crossed her arms and did her best pouting face.

"Yeah, well..." He rubbed the back of his neck and looked at his boots.

"I'm not mad at you. After all, you were gone for the last seven years. It's my sister who should shoulder most of the guilt, not you."

"Yeah, well, I still should have told you when I came back into town."

"Chase…" She waited until he looked at her. "It wasn't your place." She sighed and shook her head. "Lauren decided to head to the cabin for the rest of the weekend. I guess she's still having a hard time facing us after what she did." She shook her head. "It's not like waiting two more days is going to change how Haley and I feel."

"She went there all by herself again?" Alex saw the worried look cross his face.

"Yes, why? What is it you're not telling me?" She stood slowly, seeing his fear intensify.

"Damn." He walked off the porch and started walking towards the barn.

She caught up with him as he opened the doors. "What?" She yanked on his shoulders and turned him towards her.

"Last time we were up there, someone had broken in and been squatting at the place. Poachers, most likely, but there have been rumors about illegals hiding out and some narcotics passing through the woods. I told her I didn't want her going up there alone until we could get things checked out." He turned and started getting Buster ready.

"I'm going with you." She walked over to Haley's saddle and started getting Olivia ready.

"Does she at least have her cell phone on her?"

Alex shook her head. "She left it and Dingo here."

"Damn. You stay here. I have my cell phone and I'll call you when I know that she's safe. No use in both of us trying to make it up the hills in the dark."

Just then they heard a noise and turned to watch Tanner gallop into the barn. Chase reached out and gathered the horse's reins.

"Where's Lauren?" Alex didn't mean for it to come out as a squeal, but fear shot through her so quickly.

"I don't know." Chase reached up and touched a dark spot on the horse's mane. His hand came away covered in blood.

"Is that his blood or Lauren's?" Alex grabbed Tanner's reins, trying to get a better look.

"His, it looks like." He turned and started saddling Buster faster.

"Hang on. Don't leave just yet." She walked Tanner to his stall, then rushed into the house. Quickly gathering what he would need, she ran back with her arms full. "Here." She handed him the small box.

"What is it?" He looked down at the box.

"They're night-vision goggles." She smiled a little. "Haley got them one year. She had the strangest idea to...Well, never mind. They might come in handy. This too." She handed him a gun.

"I grabbed the shot gun from the case." He nodded towards the locked case that housed two more shotguns. He'd broken the door to get a gun and a box full of shells. "Sorry."

"This is a flare gun." She opened it and showed him the larger cartridge. "Just point and shoot. You know, in case you get into trouble and you don't have service. I'll be sitting on the porch, waiting."

"Thanks." He leaned down and placed a quick kiss on her check. "She'll be fine. Maybe she just got tossed off Tanner." Then he jumped onto Buster's back and was gone.

She watched him ride off into the dark and then the worry started taking over. Running to the house, she yelled for Haley. When her sister walked out to the porch, she filled her in on what was happening. They decided a call to the sheriff's office wouldn't hurt, and half an hour later had to explain everything again to the sheriff and two of his deputies.

Since there were no roads up to the cabin, all they could promise was to send someone tomorrow during daylight on a horse or dirt bike. That was if they had proof of a crime.

Alex and Haley watched Sheriff Stephen Miller

and his deputies leave and felt disgusted at their lack of effort. If it had been Travis, the mayor's son up there, they would have no doubt called the cavalry to ensure his safety.

Well, Lauren was more important to Alex then Travis was. She stood there looking into the darkness and praying that she wasn't too late in telling her sister how she felt.

Chase knew he was pushing Buster too hard. The horse wasn't that old, but any horse would have a hard time at full speed through the hills.

It had taken them three hours at a walk to get to the spot where they'd had lunch and another four to get to the cabin. He was determined to make it in under half that time.

He reached the clearing by the stream in just under an hour and a half. He stopped quickly and noticed Lauren's thermal lunch bag. Dismounting, he rushed over and grabbed it up, then scanned the darkness. Damn, it was too dark. Grabbing the box, he opened it and put on the night-vision goggles and looked around for a clue.

It was on his second scan that he noticed the large chunk ripped out of the tree just above his head. He looked at the ground, but couldn't see if there was any blood. Kneeling, he checked the ground, but his hand came away dry. Then he spotted something glistening off a rock a few feet away. Walking over, he touched the wetness and checked. His hand came back with red streaks.

Standing up, he screamed her name over and over. It looked more and more like she'd been thrown from Tanner and bumped her head on the rock. Where would she be? Where would she go if she was disoriented? The cabin. Could she have walked that far this quickly?" He jumped up on Buster's back and speed dialed Alex as he rode, catching her up on what he'd found.

About an hour and a half later, he smelled the fire. He knew Buster was at his limit, but he pushed the horse a little harder and made it the rest of the way in under ten minutes.

When he pulled up to the cabin, the entire place was engulfed in flames. He knew, somehow, that Lauren was inside.

Chapter Sixteen

Lauren struggled to open her eyes. She heard familiar voices and couldn't place why it was important for her to wake up. Her stomach was refusing to settle down and she knew that if the motion didn't stop she was going to be sick. When the horse came to a stop with a jerk, she lifted her head and opened her eyes. It was dark and she didn't know why that seemed wrong.

She couldn't remember where she was or what was going on. She tried desperately to remember what she'd been doing. Finally, it came back to her in a flash. She'd been shot at by the poachers. Looking up and around, she saw that she was on the back of a dark brown horse. She didn't think that it was one of hers, but she couldn't be sure. The man who sat in front of her was wearing a dark jacket and hat, covering him almost completely from her view.

She could hear two other men talking in front of them, but couldn't look around and see who or where they were.

"You can't just leave her here," someone said.

"Why not? She'll think the horse got spooked and ran off."

"It's just ain't right." She couldn't place who was speaking, but knew the voices sounded familiar.

"Shut up, both of you," the rider in front of her said. "Help me get her down. I've got a better plan."

She had an easier time placing this voice. "Larry?" She looked up to the man who had worked for her and her father for years as he twisted around and stared at her.

"Damn it. It would have been better had you stayed under." He leaned over and used his fist against her face, spiraling her into the darkness again.

When she woke next, she coughed and choked on smoke. Her hands were tied and when she tried to kick her feet, she found that they were tied as well. It was too dark to see where she was. Smoke filled the place, but so far she couldn't see any flames.

She twisted her wrists around, ripping the skin

as she tried to break free. When she couldn't budge the rope, she tried to get her feet loose. The ropes didn't budge.

She closed her eyes and forced herself to think. An image of Chase popped into her head. She was going to die and she would never get to tell him how she felt. She'd never have the opportunity to apologize to her sisters about deceiving them for so long. Tears ran down her face as she started hyperventilating.

By the time the flames lit the room, she was on the verge of passing out from the smoke. When she opened her eyes, she realized she was in her father's cabin. The whole place was burning and there was nothing she could do about it. She was going to die here, alone.

"Get up!" she told herself.

She blinked a few times, trying to steady her head.

"Lauren, get up!" It was her father's voice. The memory of the first time she'd fallen off her pony when she was seven flashed vividly in her mind.

"If you don't get up and dust yourself off, the horse wins. And you're a lot stronger and smarter than that dumb old horse, aren't you?" Her father stood over her, his hand reaching out towards hers.

She nodded and let the tears stream down her face. Her little hand reached out towards his bigger, stronger one.

"That's my girl. Now, go right over to him and tell him how you feel. Then get right back on him and ride him."

"But..."

"No, buts. You're a rancher. A dying breed. You're made of strong stuff, stronger then you will ever know. You have the power to do whatever you want in life. Don't ever let anyone tell you different. Now, walk right over, look that horse in the eyes, and tell him what you want." Her father smiled down at her, the sun streaming through his dark hair so that his face was in shadows.

Lauren sat up in the cabin. Wiggling her feet, she looked down and realized that her boots could easily be removed if she had something to help. Seeing the bunk next to her, she scooted over until it was pulling on her boot, then she pulled her legs back, dislodging it. Doing the same for the next one, she freed her legs from the ropes.

Crawling on her elbows and knees, she made her way to the front door. When she got there, she noticed the door was locked from the outside. Looking around, she knew she had to get out fast.

Picking up the small stool, she crawled towards the front window and tossed it towards the glass. It missed. She picked it up and tried again. This time it hit, shattering glass all over her head and around her. When she crawled to the opening, glass shards embedded into her hands and arms, but she couldn't feel the pain.

All that ran through her mind was staying alive so she could tell her family how she felt. Using her tied wrists, she pulled herself up to the window and looked out, gulping in a large breath of the fresh air that streamed in. The smoke swirled around her and she felt the heat from the flames at the back of the cabin.

Just then, two large hands reached in and grabbed her under her arms, hoisting her over the windowsill. The smoke had caused her eyes to water so much that she couldn't make out who was attacking her. She kicked out blindly, hoping to escape the strong arms.

"Easy, Lauren. It's me." Hearing Chase's voice, she threw her arms around his neck and helped pull her legs out of the window.

He lifted her and carried her a few yards away, where Buster stood tied to a low branch.

"Are you okay?" He ran his hands over her, checking every inch of her.

"I think so." Her eyes were fixed on the cabin. Just then half the roof caved in. Chase jumped a little then looked down at her.

"My god. I thought I'd lost you." He pulled her close and kissed her forehead.

She couldn't stop shaking. Even though the night air was warm and the heat from the fire had caused her skin to blister, her hands shook and her teeth chattered.

She pulled back and looked up at him. "It was Larry and Hewitt. I don't know who the third man was, but they shot at me." She frowned and reached for her head. "Why were they shooting at me?"

"I don't know, but let's get you back to the house so we can have you checked out." He pulled out his pocketknife and began slicing through the ropes around her wrists with a quick motion. "I'll kill them for this," he mumbled as he cut through the thick ropes.

"If I don't get to them first." She pushed her hands free and stood when he helped her. Her head spun quickly and she reached out to grab Chase, but it was too late, the darkness had taken her again.

The next time she woke, it was to light streaming in her window. When she opened her eyes, she saw Haley and Alex staring down at her, smiling.

"You scared us to death." They both looked like they'd been crying. She sat up and opened her arms so they could both engulf her together.

"I'm so sorry," she cried as they held onto her. "I should have told you about marrying Chase." She cried as they held her tight. "I should have let you guys help out more. I didn't mean to be such a…such a…"

"Control freak?" Alex pulled back and smiled down at her as tears streamed down her face.

"Well, yes." She laughed. "I'm sorry."

"We're sorry," Haley said as she sat next to her on the bed. "We should have carried more weight around here. We didn't know that you had such a large debt to repay. We would have—"

"Don't." She shook her head. "Let's not regret anything anymore." She reached up and wiped her sister's tear from her cheek. "I love you two so much, and I'd gladly do it all again to protect this place and you." She blinked a few times and looked around. "Where is Chase?"

Her sisters stilled and looked at each other.

"Alex?"

"He disappeared shortly after the doctor came and told us that you were okay. The sheriff and deputies went with him. They took a couple horses and men."

"Jimmy stayed behind," Haley said, looking down at her hands.

She closed her eyes and when she took a deep breath, she started coughing.

"The doctor says that's normal after inhaling all that smoke. The cabin is gone, but the fire was contained. Here." Alex held up a glass of water. Lauren took a large drink and felt the icy coolness soothing her sore throat.

"Any chance I can get a shower?" She looked down at herself. They'd pulled off her ruined clothes, but the grime and smoke was still embedded in her skin and hair.

"Sure, but I think a bath would be better. You've got a twisted ankle." Haley pulled back the covers to reveal a large white wrap on her left ankle.

An hour later, she felt more alive. Her sisters had propped her up on the front porch with a glass of lemonade and her cell phone. She'd tried calling Chase five times and had text him several times. So far, she hadn't heard anything back. Even the sheriff's office hadn't heard anything yet.

Alex sat with her while Haley cooked dinner.

"You know, I've given a lot of thought to what you said about Travis. I don't know if he's right for me, but I do know that I want to try and make our relationship work. It's the only thing I have going for myself at the moment."

"Alex…" She didn't know what to say. Then the memory came back to her.

"Alex, you're a rancher. We're a dying breed. We're made of strong stuff, stronger then you will ever know. You have the power to do whatever you want in life and don't ever let anyone tell you different." She took her sister's hand and watched a tear escape her eyes. "All I ever wanted, all our parents ever wanted for us was the same happiness that they felt. If Travis gives you that happiness, then I will welcome him into this family with open arms. But don't settle for anything or anyone less than you deserve. Just remember that."

"Does Chase make you feel like that?"

"Yes," she said without hesitation. "There is no doubt in my mind that I married the right man seven years ago. And as soon as he gets back here, I plan on telling him and showing him for the rest of our lives." She smiled at her sister, then pulled her close for a hug.

It was just after noon the next day when the group came upon the camp. They'd left the horses a few yards back, knowing that they needed to be as quiet as they could.

When the sheriff motioned for Chase and Grant to stay behind, Chase followed anyway. He thought he heard Grant a few feet behind him, but he was too focused on getting to Larry and the others to care.

He finally reached the clearing and he could see Larry, Hewitt, and a short Mexican man in his early forties. The three of them were arguing about a large box that sat on the ground. All three of them held rifles.

"Damn it, you should have stuck to just smuggling the cargo. No one would have been the wiser. But you had to start shooting at anything that moved." Larry turned to Hewitt. "I brought you into this operation for a reason." He looked between the men. "I've been controlling the flow for almost ten years now and you had to step in and ruin everything. Now we might have just lost our cover at Saddleback Ranch."

Larry spun and started pacing. Chase looked over at Sheriff Miller who was glaring at him fiercely. "Don't move," the older man mouthed to him.

Chase nodded in agreement. After all, the sheriff and his men were armed. They'd made sure he was not when they'd agreed to let him and Grant tag along. He wasn't stupid. He wasn't going to go running into a group of trigger-happy smugglers who were armed to the teeth. But he wasn't going to go hide under a rock, either. He wanted to make sure the men who'd almost killed Lauren were caught.

"Damn it! I knew I shouldn't have trusted someone like you." Larry's anger was focused on Hewitt. "Miguel and I have been doing just fine up until now." He pointed to the other man. "Maybe we should cut our losses." Larry pointed his pistol at Hewitt's chest. "After all, when they find all this on you, they're likely to think you were behind her death and the smuggling." Miguel smiled and pulled his weapon too.

Just then the sheriff and deputies jumped out from the bushes, screaming, "Sheriff's office. Don't move!"

Miguel dropped his weapon quickly. Hewitt backed up and tripped over the box, looking very stunned. Larry on the other hand started taking aim and firing in any direction.

The tree next to Chase exploded and he felt a sharp sting in his left arm. "Damn." He fell down behind a large stump, trying to get better cover.

Three more shots rang out, then the sheriff called over. "Is everyone alright?"

"Yeah." Chase stood up slowly and saw Larry face down in the dirt, his arms behind his back as one of the deputy cuffed him. The other two were cuffed next.

Walking over, Chase watched as the sheriff leaned over and pried open the box. Small packets of pills and white powder filled the small crate.

"Smuggling. We're seeing more and more of it around here. They bring a drug haul up from Mexico and get it as far north as they can. These hills are perfect to hide out in." The sheriff looked around and took off his hat and wiped the sweat from his brow. "Well, these boys will have the law to answer to now. Good job, Chase." The man walked away after patting him on the back.

Just then Grant came up behind him. "Damn, Chase. You've been shot." His friend looked at the blood oozing from his shoulder. He looked down and, seeing the blood, felt like laughing.

It took them a full day to drag the men back into town. By the time he made it back to the small ranch house, Chase was hot and tired and smelled ripe. It took all his energy to remove his clothes and pull himself into the tub as the water removed his soreness and pain.

He leaned his head back and closed his eyes as he felt every muscle in his body start to relax.

He must have fallen asleep, because a small sound woke him with a start. Looking up, he smiled at Lauren as she hovered over him, a breath away from his lips.

"Hello." It came out as a whisper.

"Hi, how are you feeling?" He started to sit up, but she put her hands on his shoulders, keeping him where he was.

"I'm fine. How are you?" She reached up and tucked a strand of hair behind her ear.

"Good. Better now that you're here." He reached for her face and pulled it down to his for a light kiss. Then she leaned her head against his.

"I heard you were shot." She pulled back and looked at his shoulder. He looked and saw the nasty scratch that went from his breastbone down to his upper arm.

"I wasn't really shot. I just happened to be standing too close to a tree that *was* shot." He smiled. "What'll it take to get you naked and in here with me?"

"Hmm…" She tilted her chin like she was thinking. "I'd say you've already earned whatever you've got coming." She stood up slowly and started to pull her shirt over her head. His mouth went dry as he watched her peel off every inch of her clothing.

Then she stood there for a moment, as if trying to decide how it was going to work. "I'm not sure this is a wise decision." She braced herself on the ledge and put one foot in. "I do have a twisted ankle. Oh, but it does feel good." She smiled and stepped in with the other foot, straddling his hips as she slid down and sat on his chest. Leaning forward she kissed him as his hands roamed over her backside.

Sitting up a little, he gripped her hips and forced her all the way down on his desire as she moaned with pleasure. "No barriers this time, wife," he moaned.

"No, never again." She smiled as her hips started moving. The water splashed over the edge of the tub, sending water running over the floor and his clothing. Neither of them noticed as it lapped rhythmically as they slowly gained speed until both of them were panting and out of breath.

"More," he said as his fingers dug into her hips.

Her hands pulled his head to hers as she took the kiss deeper. He couldn't get enough. She was going too slow. He pulled her up and off, then stood and stepped out of the tub, then turned and picked her up and carried her to the bed. Laying her down gently, he covered her with his body and entered her quickly as her legs wrapped around him.

"More." This time it was her who had demanded it. His thrusts grew deeper as he stroked her inner muscles. His mouth played with her erect nipples, causing pleasure to flow through every pore. When she leaned her head back and screamed his name, he was two seconds behind her in his release.

They lay there, breathing heavily until the air cooled their skin. He reached over and pulled the comforter over them both, enjoying the feel of her snuggling up to his chest.

"Chase." She ran her hand lightly over his chest. "Back when I was locked in the cabin, I thought I wouldn't get a chance to tell you how I feel." She leaned up and looked down into his eyes.

"I think you just did, darling." He smiled at her and gently put a strand of her hair behind her ear, so he could see her face clearly.

She smiled down at him. "Yes, but I think you and I both need to hear the words." She sighed as his other hand skimmed over her hip. "I love the way you make me feel. What you do to me when you look at me." Her smile fell away. "The thought of not being with you scares me now. I want to be really married to you. To grow old with you and have children with you."

He sat up, pulling her with him. "Lauren, I know this is a little late, but will you marry me?" She laughed and nodded her head. He smiled and took her face in his hands. "I love you. I've loved you for over seven years." She smiled when he said this. "I want to keep loving you."

"Yes, I love you, too." She leaned in and kissed him. "Move into the house and help me make it a home."

He smiled and took her lips again, pulling her back down to the bed just as the sun set behind the hills.

Jill Sanders

Epilogue

"You've ruined me." Lauren leaned back in her chair and looked across the table at Chase.

"How do you figure?" He smiled over at her and took a drink of his beer.

"I'm going to expect presents like this every year from now on." She nodded to her new diamond wedding ring. It was his gift to her on their eight-year anniversary.

They were sitting out back on the deck of the house shortly after dinner. Her sisters had quickly disappeared after eating, taking the dirty dishes and plates with them.

"Good." He stood and held out his hand. "Take a walk with me."

It had been six months since the cabin had burned down. The dark spot where it used to be still sat empty. They'd talked about rebuilding it, but wanted to focus on fixing the house up first.

They had been more successful at the auction last year than expected and had had so much fun in Tyler together that they'd stayed an extra few days as a mini vacation, almost like a honeymoon.

When she'd returned home, she was shocked to see a fresh coat of paint on the house, all new windows, and a new water heater, something she now couldn't live without. Over the course of the next months, Chase had put so much effort into fixing up the house that at this point it almost looked new.

Reaching out, she took his hand and smiled as he pulled her into his arms for a quick kiss. Then he turned and with her hand in his, started walking into the fields.

When they reached a small hill, he turned her and they stood hand in hand looking at the house with the sun setting behind them. The new windows gleamed in the dying sunlight. The fresh paint and new roof made the place look brand new.

"It's a great place," he said and pulled her into his arms.

"Yes, it is." She sighed and turned in his arms, wrapping her arms around him.

When he started moving back and forth, she leaned her head against his chest. "What are you doing?"

"Dancing." He chuckled.

"There's no music." She looked up and smiled at him.

"There doesn't need to be any to dance in our fields." He took her hand in his, putting his other on her waist and spinning her in a circle. Then he dipped her low and kissed her until her head spun.

When he stood her back up, she looked into his eyes and knew that she was right where she wanted to be, in the arms of the perfect husband.

Jill Sanders

Taming Alex - Preview
Prologue

Alex stood in the grocery store. She looked up and down the aisles before slipping the small figurine into her coat pocket. Oh, she knew that stealing was wrong, but since God had taken away her mother a few months ago, she figured He owed her one. Besides, her ma had promised to buy the small horse for her on her seventh birthday. That day had come and gone last week. She'd prayed and prayed that her mother would get her the small metal horse from heaven somehow, but after she'd opened the last of her presents at her small birthday party and there was still no horse, she'd known exactly what she needed to do.

It was the first day of school, and she'd convinced Lauren to walk with her to the Grocery Stop after school. The Grocery Stop was Fairplay's only market, and was only a few blocks from their school. They had a whole hour to wait for their pa before he'd be able to come and pick them up.

Getting her sister to leave her alone in the aisle where the small statues sat in a large glass case took a lot of talking. Finally, Alex had told her big sister that she had to use the bathroom. When Lauren wanted to come into the small room with her, Alex had thrown a fit.

"I'm a big girl. I don't want you watching me." She'd stood there with her hands on her hips, just like their ma used to do. Her sister finally told her that she'd wait for her at the front counter and left her alone. She waited in the bathroom long enough so that her sister could make it up front. Then she peeked out the crack of the door to make sure that she had disappeared. She tiptoed down the aisle and pocketed the horse smoothly. She hadn't counted on a hand dropping onto her shoulder.

"You aren't supposed to do that."

Alex spun around to see Grant "Do-gooder" Holton standing behind her. Grant was the same age as Alex and had earned the nickname by being the town's biggest tattletale. He thought that just because his daddy was the town's hotshot lawyer that he had to tell everyone else what to do. All the other kids at school made fun of him about it.

Grant was a little taller than she was. Then again, almost everyone was taller than she was. Her mother had said that she was a small statue. Alex didn't know what that meant, but she wasn't happy that Haley, her little sister, was already taller than she was.

She looked across the aisle at Grant. He was chubby and wore glasses that were always sliding off his nose. He was always wearing his best church clothes, or so Alexis always thought, since she'd never seen him in a pair of jeans or a T-shirt, ever. His hair always looked like he had just combed it, and she had never seen him dirty.

Alex thought the glasses made him look smarter and desperately wished that she needed glasses so she would do better in math class, but the doctor had said she had perfect eyes. Grant's hair was a shade darker than her own blonde, but his had a curl to it. She wished she had curly hair, since her hair was so thin it was hard to braid.

She wrapped her small fingers around the cool metal of the horse in her pocket. "I'm not giving it back." She stomped her foot. "God owes it to me since he took my mama away." Her eyes started to water up and her bottom lip quivered.

"Stealing is a sin. Besides, you can go to jail if they catch you." His face started turning a darker shade of red. "I'm gonna have to tell."

She reached out and grabbed his coat before he could walk away. "Don't you dare, Grant Holton." She looked up at him and thought of a way out of this mess. "If...if you promise not to tell anyone..." Her little mind desperately reached for some means to hold him to a promise. "I promise..." He waited, his big blue eyes looking into hers, and she blurted out. "I'll let you kiss me."

Grant's eyes got bigger behind his glasses. He thought about it a moment, then said, "For real?" He looked around.

What was it to her? She'd seen her ma and pa do

it lots of times. She didn't see what all the fuss was about, since it looked sloppy and gross, but if it got Grant to shut up about the statue, she'd tolerate it.

She nodded her head her eyes and smiled. "Sure."

"On the lips?" His head tilted as he waited.

"Why not? Is it a deal?"

Grant thought about it for another second, then nodded his head as he pushed up his glasses. When he took a step closer to her, she almost lost her nerve. Instead, she closed her eyes and puckered up her lips like she'd seen her mother do. When his lips touched hers she wanted to pull back and wipe her mouth off, but then something happened. She started to like it. His lips were soft and not wet, after all. They felt like feathers tickling her lips and she actually felt her feet and hands start to tingle.

After what seemed like years, he finally pulled away, a huge smile on his lips. Then he turned and rushed down the aisle and out the front door without a word. She hadn't even made sure he was going to stick to their bargain.

"Come on, Alexis. Dad's here," her sister called from the front of the store.

Smiling, she held onto the small horse in her pocket and walked towards the front. She thought about kissing Grant and decided that she liked kissing. She wanted to do it again and as often as

she could. And with as many boys as she wanted
to.

Jill Sanders

Chapter One

Ten years later...

Alex held her breath as her father's coffin was lowered into the ground. Her world was shattered, again. Looking over to Haley, she wondered what would happen to the three of them. After all, Haley was only fourteen. She reached over and grabbed Lauren's hand in her own, then held onto Haley's.

The three of them stood and watched as their father's coffin sank lower into the red dirt at the church's cemetery, in the plot next to their mother's.

Lauren's eyes closed for just a second until her sister dropped her hand and walked over to place a white rose into the hole. It landed softly on the coffin. Lauren turned and nodded to her, then she followed. As she dropped her rose, she stood and said her goodbyes to the man who had done his best to raise the three girls alone and make them happy.

When she turned, Haley walked up and stood next to the hole. Alex couldn't stand it anymore. She turned and walked quickly towards a group of trees. Even though it was spring, the heat was almost too much for her to bear. Here in the shade she could feel the breeze, and she felt like she could finally breathe.

Leaning against the trunk of a large oak tree, she closed her eyes and focused on taking slow breaths. She'd been staying at Cheryl Lynn's house the night that Lauren had found their father on the floor of his room. She should have stayed home that weekend. If she had only stayed…

"Hey." She looked up into Grant's deep blue eyes. He looked pretty much the same as he always had, but his sandy hair was a little longer and he'd gotten new glasses. The wire rims suited his face a little better. He had a slight case of acne on his round face, but his clothes were still spotless.

"Hey." She continued to lean against the tree, crossing her arms over her chest. She started to feel cold and wished for the warmth of the sun again.

"I'm sorry about your dad." He looked down at his shiny boots and kicked a pebble. Grant's father and her father had been best friends since childhood. Even their mothers had been friends, since they'd all grown up in the small town. "I sure hope you don't have to sell your ranch or anything."

Her shoulders came off the tree and she looked at him. "Why would we?" She frowned.

He looked up from his boot and stared at her. "I don't know, I just overheard my pa talking about some money problems your pa had and how Lauren wasn't old enough to take care of you and your sister and a run a ranch at the same time." He raised then dropped his shoulders.

"She's not all by herself. She has Haley and me." She took a step closer to him.

"Well, I hope you're right. I'm leaving at the end of this year. I was accepted into Harvard." He smiled real big.

Her chin dropped and she said, "We're only seventeen."

"I know. I finished all my credits for high school over the summer and my dad and I sent in applications. Can you believe it?" He stuck his hands into his pant pockets.

"You're only seventeen," she repeated.

"Are you gonna miss me?" It came out as a whisper, and Alex didn't hear it. Her mind was stuck on the fact that she was seventeen and now both her parents were gone and she was facing the possibility of losing the only home she'd ever known.

Then she looked over her shoulder and frowned a little. She saw that Grant's father and Mr. Graham, her father's other best friend, were talking to Lauren next to their truck.

Walking away without saying goodbye, she rushed over to where Haley stood next to her friends and grabbed her hand. "We need to go."

Haley nodded and followed her. They walked up to their sister together.

"We're ready to go home." Alex glared at Mr. Graham and Mr. Holton, who quickly turned their eyes to the ground. Chase, Mr. Graham's son, was standing next to them. He smiled slightly and nodded his head, then the girls left.

The drive home was quiet. Alex wanted to ask her sister what her plans were, but knew it wasn't the right time. Lauren was a week shy of her nineteenth birthday. She was old enough to legally take care of Alex and Haley, that much she knew. She didn't know anything about the money problems their father was having, or even if the ranch had been left to Lauren. Lauren would know all that. After all, for the last few years, Lauren had been helping their father out with the big place.

When the truck turned into their long driveway, Alex looked at their three-story house in the distance. The once freshly painted white building could stand a new coat. The roof had just been replaced a few years back. Alex knew the old place had its problems, but she wouldn't have traded it for any other house in the county.

"Lauren?" She looked at her sister as she parked the truck, wanting to ask so many questions. Just then, Haley pushed out of the truck and raced towards the barn.

Lauren looked at her and smiled. "I'll get her." Lauren left Alex alone in the truck as she raced after their little sister.

Alex's eyes watered. This was really happening. They were going to lose the ranch. Most likely, they would be split up too. Where were they going to live? What was going to happen to them?

Alex rushed into the house and slowly walked around the place. She was trying to memorize every small detail—all the furnishings, the look and the smell of the place. She ended up in their father's room and when she sat on his bed, she began to softly cry.

It was just like when their mother had died. If she hadn't stopped to grab the cookies, Haley wouldn't have snuck out and run upstairs. Then their mother wouldn't have gone and gotten her. They would have all made it to the shelter in time. Instead, the three girls had had to watch in horror as the tornado ripped their mother into the darkness and out of their lives forever.

If she would have just stayed home this last weekend, their father would still be alive. It was all her fault. Dropping to his bed, she inhaled his rich musky scent and cried until her heart and head hurt. She must have fallen asleep, because when she woke up, it was dark outside the window.

Standing up, she went into her own room and changed into her jeans and work shirt. She knew the horses needed feeding and it had been her job for the last few years. When she walked out to the barn, she saw that the task had already been done. Her shoulders slumped and she sat down in the soft hay, feeling like she'd let her family down again. She made a pact right then and there that she would never let her sisters down again.

Over the course of the next few months, it became apparent that Lauren had everything under control around the ranch. Her sister had even taken over her and Haley's chores, telling them both that they needed to focus on their studies instead.

Lauren had driven Alex down to get her driver's license, and had given her the old red Honda to drive her and Haley to school every day. She didn't mind driving them around all the time, since she knew Lauren was busy. They had sat down the next week and Lauren had told them that all the bills were paid and that no one was going to take the ranch away. Even better, she had signed the official paperwork with Mr. Graham that stated that she had full custody of Alex and Haley. Lauren was their legal guardian. No one was going to separate the three of them, ever.

Alex relaxed into a schedule, knowing that her

sister would take care of whatever popped up around the ranch. After a few months, guilt settled in when she noticed how much her sister actually did around the place, and she started doing things without being told to. She asked Jamella down at Mama's for a part-time job and picked up as many hours as she could, just to pay for her gas. But she started making extra money and would always leave it in Lauren's office for her. Her sister never mentioned it, so she continued to give her half of her weekly paycheck. Even Haley picked up on what was going on and started helping out with the animals more and more.

But then just a year later, Alex started dating Travis, and her life had a new purpose—to do everything she could to become Mrs. Travis Nolan.

Almost Eight years later...

Alex stood in the dark parking lot, feeling like kicking something or someone. How could he do this to her again? She looked around the almost-empty lot and felt like screaming.

Instead, she tossed the beer bottle she was

holding and smiled when the glass shattered all over his blue truck. The engagement ring on her left finger sparkled in the parking lot's dim lighting. She felt like ripping it off her finger and throwing it as well, but stopped herself before she could follow through. It was her birthday and Travis had gotten so drunk. He was now passed out behind the wheel of his precious truck again. Even the shattering of her beer bottle over his windshield had done little to wake him.

Over the last few months, she'd told herself she was going to really evaluate their relationship. She'd made the decision after Lauren and Chase had sprung it on everyone that they had gotten married the day after their father's funeral. Lauren had married him out of desperation to get out from under a crushing debt, but now they were completely happy about it. Chase had moved into the house and they acted like newlyweds, which she supposed they were since Chase had been gone for the last seven years.

She walked up to Travis' truck and looked at him through his open window. He was still as handsome as the day she'd fallen for him. He had the classic rugged cowboy look that she'd always swooned over. Even the cleft in his chin melted her heart. But lately, his actions were speaking more loudly to her, and she was falling farther and farther away from that soft gooey feeling he had always invoked in her.

She turned and leaned on the truck, crossing her

arms over her chest. The steamy, summer night air caused her white blouse to stick to her skin and she desperately wished for a shower. Her hair was plastered to her neck and face, since she and her friends had spent the last few hours line dancing at The Rusty Rail, the local bar and dance hall. Everyone had come out to celebrate her birthday. A stack of her presents filled the back of Travis' truck. She smiled when she looked back at the packages. Travis had promised her that he wouldn't drink too much tonight, since she hated it when he got so drunk that he started getting rude. He'd never raised a finger towards her, but he did get a little mean with his words and, a few times, she'd had to walk to her friend's house and spend the night instead of letting him drive her home.

"Hey, baby." She turned to see him smiling at her. "Happy birthday." He looked at her funny, then leaned through the window and puked on her white boots.

"Travis!" She jumped back just in time to only get a little splatter.

"Oh, I'm sorry, baby." He started to get out of the truck.

"You're sorry? You've ruined my whole night. You were too busy drinking and hanging out with your buddies to even dance with me." She stepped away from him when he tried to reach over and pull her close. "You forgot to bring my present and, to be honest, I don't think you remembered to get one in the first place."

"I did, honest. It's at my dad's place." She could see the lie in his eyes, which only hurt her more.

"Now you're so drunk you've ruined my favorite boots. Hand me your keys." She held out her hand and tapped her foot. "I'm driving you home, then going home."

He shook his head, then grabbed it and almost toppled over. "No! You know I don't let anyone drive this beauty except me." He tapped his truck and his hand came away wet. "God damn it. Someone's throwing bottles at her." He rushed over and looked at the shattered glass and the almost dry beer.

"I did." She crossed her arms and waited.

"You?" He turned and glared at her. "You scratched her. Why would you do that? It's going to cost hundreds of dollars to buff this out." He was running his fingers over a tiny scratch on the hood. Then he turned towards her with a slight smile on his face. "There goes your birthday present. I'm taking it back to the store so I can pay for this damage."

"Whatever. You know you didn't buy me anything." She started walking away.

"Where are you going? Get back here," he called after her.

"I'm going to Cheryl Lynn's," she called over her shoulder.

"Don't, baby. Come back. I'll give you a ride back to my place." It was an old argument that he had never won. She had never and would never spend the night at his trashed-out apartment over his father's garage. Travis kept the place so dirty, that she'd never even really stepped foot in it. The dirty apartment wasn't the only reason she hadn't spent the night at his place. She couldn't explain it, but she just didn't want to stay there, with him. At least, she talked herself into adding, until they were married.

"Alex, get your butt back here." She knew he'd try a couple different tactics. The next one would be to drive by her and yell at her through the open window. He would start calling her names as she walked, but she always ignored it all, telling herself it was the beer talking.

The next day she would get some flowers and he'd come by and they'd make up. It was their pattern.

But as she walked farther down the dark street towards Cheryl Lynn's place, he didn't drive by her. She turned and looked back at the parking lot and noticed he'd gotten back into the truck.

Probably passed out again, she told herself as she kept walking. Cheryl's place was two miles away, an easy enough walk in the day. But tonight, with the moon only a sliver in the sky, she kept tripping over rocks and clumps of grass along the narrow road.

Less than two minutes later, lights hit her and she stopped and waited until he pulled up next to her. But instead of Travis' truck, a dark black Ford pulled up. When the tinted windows lowered, Grant Holton called out.

"Alexis West is that you? What on earth are you doing walking along a dark road at this time of night? I could have hit you." It was too dark to see him fully, but she knew that voice anywhere.

"Shut up, Grant." She walked over and pulled open the door to his truck. She was happy when his passenger seat was empty, and she climbed up to sit next to him. "Drive me to Cheryl Lynn's place, would you?" She crossed her arms over her chest and frowned out the front window.

Grant had come home earlier this year and even though the chubby, zit-covered, glasses-wearing geek had been replaced with a skinny, clear-skinned hunk, to her he was the same old Grant "Do-gooder" Holton. Always trying to fix everyone else's problems.

"Travis isn't going to drive you home?" he asked. She turned and glared at him.

"No," she said, then watched as he turned back and looked out the window. He had yet to start driving, and she was slowly getting mad.

"Hmm," he said, and she watched as he looked out the back of his truck towards the Rusty Rail.

"What?" She turned in her seat and glared at

him in the dark.

He shook his head. "Nothing."

"Grant Holton, you're lying." Everyone could always tell when he had something to tell. The whole town knew he couldn't hide anything from anyone.

"It's nothing." He reached over and pulled on her seat belt. When his arm brushed against her chest, she held her breath. She knew he hadn't meant the move to mean anything, but still the featherlight touch shocked her.

"Sorry," he mumbled and dropped his arm. "I don't start driving until the seat belts are on."

She rolled her eyes and reached down to finish locking the seat belt into place.

"Are you going to tell me what secret you have?" She looked over at him.

"No secret," he said and then finally put his truck into gear.

"Fine, don't tell me. It's not like I care anyway." She looked out the front window, feeling sad.

"I'm sorry you two broke up on your birthday," he said, causing her head to swivel towards him.

"We didn't break up. Who told you we broke up?" Her voice hitched.

"It's just...I thought..." There was a moment of silence and then he cleared his throat. "I just assumed."

"Why?" She grabbed onto his arm, digging her nails into his skin a little.

He looked over at her, then back towards the road. He remained silent until he pulled the truck off the road into the old train station parking lot.

"When I walked out to leave the Rusty Rail, I saw him and Savannah Douglas making out in the parking lot against his truck." His voice held a hint of sadness, and his eyes, at least what she could see in the darkness, held concern.

"Who put you up to this?" She crossed her arms over her chest again.

"What?" He blinked and leaned back a little. He looked like he was waiting for her to slap him across the face. Instead, she started laughing.

"Oh, this is rich. Did Billy put you up to this?" She stopped chuckling and wiped a tear from her eye. "Billy's always trying to get me to believe that Travis and Savannah have had a thing in the past."

Grant shook his head. "I'm sorry, Alex." He turned and looked out the front window, then was quiet. They sat there for a few seconds before she jumped out of the truck and started quickly walking back to the Rusty Rail.

She heard the truck door slam behind her, then Grant grabbed her shoulders. She swung out, connecting her fist with his chin as tears blinded her eyes.

"That bastard!" she screamed. "He promised it was just a one-time deal." She struck out again, blindly, only connecting with air as his hands wrapped gently around her wrists. "We'd broken up and he was drunk, he said..." She kicked at Grant and tried to get her wrists free, only to be pulled up close against a rock-hard body as muscular arms wrapped around her. Her grief was too much and as the dam behind her eyes finally cut loose, she heard Grant whisper words of kindness into her hair as she cried her heart out against his chest.

Other books by Jill Sanders

The Pride Series
Finding Pride – Pride Series #1
Discovering Pride – Pride Series #2
Returning Pride – Pride Series #3
Lasting Pride – Pride Series #4
Serving Pride – Prequel to Pride Series #5
Red Hot Christmas – A Pride Christmas #6
My Sweet Valentine – Pride Series #7
Summer Crush – Pride Series #8

The Secret Series
Secret Seduction – Secret Series #1
Secret Pleasure – Secret Series #2
Secret Guardian – Secret Series #3
Secret Passions – Secret Series #4
Secret Identity – Secret Series #5
Secret Sauce – Secret Series #6

The West Series
Loving Lauren – West Series #1
Taming Alex – West Series #2
Holding Haley – West Series #3
Missy's Moment – West Series #4
Breaking Travis - West Series #5
Roping Ryan - West Series #6
Wild Bride – West Series #7

For a complete list of books, visit JillSanders.com

This is a work of fiction. Names, characters, places, and incidents are either the product of the author's imagination or are used fictitiously, and any resemblance to actual persons, living or dead, business establishments, events, or locales is entirely coincidental.

Follow Jill Sanders online at:
Web: www.jillsanders.com
Twitter: jillmsanders
Facebook: jillsandersbooks

LOVING LAUREN
ISBN: 978-1497346215
Copyright © 2014 Jill Sanders
Copyeditor: Erica Ellis – inkdeepediting.com

About the Author

Jill Sanders is the New York Times and USA Today bestselling author of the Pride Series, the Secret Series, and the West Series romance novels. Having sold over 150,000 books within six months of her first release, she continues to lure new readers with her sweet and sexy stories. Her books are available in every English-speaking country, available in audio books, and are now being translated into six different languages.

Born as an identical twin in a large family, she was raised in the Pacific Northwest. She later relocated to Colorado for college and a successful IT career before discovering her talent as a writer. She now makes her home in charming rural Florida where she enjoys the beach, swimming, hiking, wine tasting, and, of course, writing.